Perfect Lie

TERESA MUMMERT

Prologue

I cried again tonight. I tried to hold back the tears, but they used that word. That sickening word that opens the floodgates of my emotions. *Worthless*. It wasn't that I viewed my tears as a weakness; it was that I knew what they'd said was true. I was a nothing. No one looked forward to seeing me in the morning. No one laid his head on his pillow at night to dream of me. I existed by pure accident, and no one would let me forget how unwanted I was.

I woke with a thin layer of sweat covering my body as chills ran through me. Pushing the dyed-blond hair from my forehead, I struggled to slow my breathing. My eyes darted to my cell phone beside my bed as I contemplated calling Marie. My vision slowly adjusted to my dark, cramped bedroom. I wasn't in Mississippi anymore. I was someone new in a new town. I wasn't living that nightmare that plagued me every time I closed my eyes.

Sometimes love burns so hot in your veins that it consumes all rational thought. You become a walking shell that can no longer function without your significant other whispering into your soul, telling your heart to beat.

I sighed as I slid out of my single bed, my covers falling over the edge and pooling at my feet. The hardwood floor creaked and moaned as I tiptoed my way into the kitchen in my oversize anarchy T-shirt that nearly swallowed me. I should have thrown it away after high school. Marie would have a fit if she knew I still hung on to it—to the memory of what could have been. But I couldn't force myself to say good-bye to Brock and not blame myself for the way things had fallen apart.

Chapter One

One Day at a Time

"Was that you I heard creeping around last night?" Trish asked, as she pulled open the fridge and scavenged for something to eat. Trish Wentworth, the epitome of everything I'd hated in high school. I stifled a yawn as I stretched my arms over my head and watched her sift through our nearly empty kitchen.

"I was getting a drink. It's important to stay hydrated," I replied dryly.

Trish's head spun around, and her blue eyes narrowed as she tried to decide if I was being a smartass or finally listening to some of her beauty advice. Her bright-blond hair whipped across her face as she moved. It shone like gold atop her porcelain skin, and I sank lower into my seat, knowing I should take her advice more seriously. Girls dreamed of looking half as beautiful as Trish, with her pixie-like nose and high cheekbones. Disney couldn't create a princess as beautiful. Of course none of them were raging alcoholics who loved to get high.

"Your skin is a little dry. Wouldn't hurt for you to moisturize." She shrugged as her head disappeared through the open door. I rolled my eyes as I fought the urge to kick her in the ass and send her face first into a leftover meat loaf.

"I'll keep that in mind." I yawned again, this time moaning loudly.

"Beauty sleep isn't just a phrase. It would do you some good."

"Thanks again, Trish. You're a fount of wisdom this morning." I couldn't hide my frustration after a night of nightmares.

"Whatever. I have class in an hour, but I'm skipping it to hit the gym. Wanna come?"

I snorted, my hand covering my mouth as soon as the sound escaped. "Last time I went to that god-awful place, I fell off the treadmill, and you said I wasn't allowed to go back." I couldn't help the laugh that followed. I hated the gym almost as much as I hated pretending to be perfect. It was exhausting. "I have a meeting today anyway."

Trish eyed me for a moment but nodded as she left to go back down the hallway, a bottle of water in her hand. "Ugh. Who puts this much time into their future?" She shook her head as she disappeared into her room. I rolled my eyes, quietly mocking her as I picked at the polish that peeled from my thumbnail. I don't know if Trish believed my blatant lie about the meetings, or if she genuinely didn't care what I was up to every Friday morning.

I'd vaguely explained the meetings as being a group of college students who gathered to chat about how women were being treated in the work force. I groaned loudly as I stood from the table and stretched, my favorite shirt riding up over my belly button. I was outgrowing it, and the thought of it not fitting one day set off my anxiety. I tried to focus on the novel I'd been reading, trying to get lost in the world of the characters in my head as I made my way to my room to get dressed for the day.

I absent-mindedly pulled on a worn pair of fitted jeans and a navy-blue tank top. I gathered my hair in messy ponytail as I stared at myself in the mirror over my dresser. I had changed a lot over the last year, and I barely recognized myself. My hair, once a dull brown, was now vibrant blond. I had traded my dark eyeliner for rosy cheeks and a pale-pink gloss on my lips. Still I was a plain Jane by anyone's standards. Freckles dusted over my nose and across the apples of my cheeks. My lips were thinner than I would like, and my eyes were big and wide like a Kewpie doll's.

I slid my feet into my matching blue sandals and grabbed my bag, an old army-green tote with a strap that was long enough to wear across my body.

"I'm leaving," I called out, but Trish didn't respond as I shuffled to the door of our cramped apartment then pulled it closed behind me and locked it.

The warm air assaulted me as I stepped into the bright Orlando sun. I chose this state to go to college because it was far from Mississippi, and people who lived this close to the ocean were supposed to be happy. At least that's what movies and television had led me to believe. It also happened to be where my uncle lived, even though I avoided him at all costs. He still had that look in his eye whenever he talked to me, and I couldn't stand the pity. I regretted ever showing up on his doorstep and burdening him with my baggage. I just wanted to forget and move on.

Marie's office was only a few blocks away, so I didn't need to bother catching a bus. I enjoyed the walk. It was the only time I could really be alone, though I always felt I was, even in the most crowded rooms. It was hot, but there wasn't as much humidity compared to back home, so it was still easy to breathe, not like a ton of bricks pressing against my chest as I inhaled.

I climbed the white iron staircase outside the small pale-pink stucco building as my breathing quickened. I tried, as always, to talk myself out of going through with my appointment. The door popped open, and June stuck out her head from behind the door with a large smile.

"Planning your escape, Delilah?" She winked as she pushed the door open farther so I could slip in past her.

I smiled back as I stepped inside and closed my eyes. The temperature was a good fifteen degrees cooler than outside, and it felt incredible. I made my way to the three folding chairs along the wall, but June stopped me before I could sit down.

"She's already waiting for you."

Of course she was waiting. I had taken my sweet time walking over here and was now ten minutes late. I grabbed the handle to Marie's office and shoved it open.

"You're late," she said with a playful smile as she brushed her shoulder-length chestnut hair off her shoulder, revealing the birthmark that ran from her left ear and disappeared below the collar of her blouse. She used to cover it with makeup, but after a few sessions, she no longer tried to hide it, which made me feel more at ease. She trusted me with her secret, and I felt I could trust her with mine.

"You didn't see that in your crystal ball?" I teased, and Marie shook her head, her cheeks blushing to the color of the mark.

"I told you about that psychic in confidence." She gave me a hard look but was still smiling. "And she didn't say I was a mind reader—although it would make my job a whole lot easier." I closed the door behind me and made my way to the black leather chair across from her as she wrote something in the note-book that rested on her lap.

"Right. You like to sleep with dead people," I replied, straight faced. I loved poking fun at her.

"Delilah! She said I was a necromancer in my past life. They *talk* to dead people." She shook her head as she laughed from deep in her stomach, revealing the laugh lines around her mouth. "What you're referring to is necrophilia and absolutely disgusting."

"That makes me feel a little better." I smirked as my eyes danced over the caricature of her that hung in a simple wood frame over a dusty fake palm plant. It wasn't an over-the-top room, and it reminded me more of a small living room than an office. Marie added little personal touches all around. I suppose this was to make people feel more comfortable and at home, but it bordered on unprofessional. Still there was something about Marie, the way she tucked a leg under herself as she sat, as if we were old friends; the way she laughed inappropriately at my sarcastic humor instead of judging me.

"It was just in good fun anyway." She waved her hand.

"Please don't tell me you went to that crackerjack trying to find out when some guy was going to come sweep you off your feet."

"Some of my colleagues thought it would be fun. That's all. I don't take any stock in what those psychics have to say."

"*Psychics*? As in plural? How many have you seen? You're never gonna get hitched if you're hanging out in seedy palm readers' basements."

"What's with your fascination with my love life?"

"It'd be nice if one of us was getting some action." I let my shoulders fall as I looked at her. "Any guy would be lucky to have you."

"Thanks." She picked up her glass of water and took a sip. "But I just don't think it's in the cards."

I picked at her playfully. "Marie, did you just make a joke? Was that a tarot-card joke? I want to make sure. I'd hate to miss it."

"All right. All right. Enough about my nonexistent love life. We're here to chat about you."

"I almost didn't come," I said, as I picked up chess piece from the small glass table between us and studied it.

Marie shrugged and glanced down at my hand, watching as I turned it over between my fingers. "I'm trying to learn how to play, but I haven't been able to really get into it. Do you play?"

I shook my head and put the piece back on the board as I relaxed in my seat.

"You never played any games with Brock?" she asked casually, as she pulled a pack of mints from her pocket and popped one into her mouth. She held the container out to me, but I waved it away.

"Not really. Just a little at the shelter. How's quitting going?" That was my lame attempt to change the subject.

"I haven't had a cigarette in three days."

"Congrats!" I was genuinely proud of her. My mother was a smoker, and no matter how hard she tried, she never could kick the habit. I think she viewed it as the world's slowest suicide attempt.

"Tell me about the shelter."

I sighed as I glanced at the large window along the back wall. Raindrops splattered against the glass, which was normal for this area. It seemed to rain every five minutes, but usually it just made the heat worse. My eyes focused on a small pink potted flower as I thought about Brock.

"I met Brock at the shelter."

"Why were you there?" she asked, as her gaze followed mine to the window before settling back on me.

"I ran away. I just needed a break. Mom and I had been fighting as usual. She grounded me, which didn't mean much. Our arguments were getting worse, and I needed to get away from her."

"Where did you go? Did you have a plan?"

"No. It wasn't like that. I didn't really care where I ended up, as long as I was away from her—away from everyone."

"You said before they found you more than an hour from home. How did you get so far away in one night?"

"I had the weird pervy guy down the street take me." I laughed nervously, knowing how stupid that sounded. "Then the cops found me and told me my mother didn't want me to come back home. She was afraid I'd run away again. So instead they took me to the shelter."

Marie didn't scold me; she only cocked her head to the side and shook it slightly. "Tell me about meeting Brock."

I swallowed hard as I got lost in the memory of the boy who changed everything.

"Whatchya writin'?"

I glanced up to see a pair of gray eyes.

"A novel." I covered my notebook with my free arm so the stranger couldn't read anything I wrote.

He laughed as he shook his head. "You been inside one day, and you're already writin' your memoirs?" he joked with a thick Boston accent.

"No. I'm a writer—at least I wanted to be before I ended up in this place." My eyes scanned his dark buzzed hair and haunting gray eyes.

"You don't just end up in a place like this, sweetheart. You had to be a bad girl to get in here."

"Would you believe I was innocent?" I tried to suppress my grin as I narrowed my eyes at him. He didn't, and I caught a flash of his perfectly white teeth and the deep dimples that settled into his tanned cheeks. His jaw was strong and square, like a statue of a Roman gladiator. The only imperfection was a thin scar that cut across his right eyebrow, which only made me focus on his intense stare.

"Not a chance."

My breathing caught as I was trapped under his gaze. He grabbed the chair in front of him and sat directly across from me. His shirt was pulled tautly across his chest, and I had the urge to reach out and run my hands over his muscles.

"This isn't prison. It isn't even juvie. It's some dumb-shit place for our parents to get rid of us for a while and not feel like they're the bad guys. Don't be too hard on yourself."

"Yeah, well, it worked, and it's hard not to blame myself." I rolled my eyes as I doodled stars on my paper.

He sat back in his chair, stretching his long legs under the table. His foot bumped against mine, and I quickly pulled my feet back under my chair. "What did you do to get in here?" he asked. "You get a B instead of an A?"

I glanced up at him, any trace of humor gone from my expression. "I was born."

He snorted, but his smile fell as he leaned forward and propped himself on his elbows. "I really want to know."

"I just told you." I flipped my notebook closed and stood from my chair.

"I was a mistake that my mother has been trying to correct since I was born." I stalked off before the tears that threatened to fall made *it past my lashes. As soon as I reached my room, I curled up on my bed and let the sobs rip from my chest. I'd never told anyone that my mother wished I hadn't been born. It was a secret that ate me alive from the inside like a disease. A family friend had raped her when she was fifteen years old. Her parents—my grandparents—were deeply religious and told her it would be a sin to have an abortion. Of course, once I was born, I was the ugly spot on the family tree. They wanted nothing to do with me. They left me with a child, a victim of rape who knew nothing about being a parent or an adult. My mother spent years struggling to survive, all the while secretly wishing I would disappear.*

"I didn't mean to upset you," he said.

I pulled myself from my memories and glanced up at the boy through blurry eyes.

"Too late." I sniffled as I sat up, wrapping my arms around my legs.

"I'm Brock, the asshole," he said, as he crossed the room slowly and sat down on my roommate's bed.

"I'm Delilah, the mistake." I laughed nervously as I wiped my hand across my cheek. Brock also laughed, humorlessly.

"That's a nice name."

"My friends call me 'Lie.' Not really. I don't have any." I rolled my eyes, wishing the room would swallow me whole.

Brock shook his head and sat next to me on my bed. I slid over, not liking being so close to someone I didn't know, and wondered what his motive was. No one was ever nice to me just for the sake of being nice. He had to want something.

"I stole a car and disappeared for a few weeks," he confessed with a laugh as he ran his hand along his strong jaw.

"Accidents happen." I shrugged as I let my legs hang over the edge of the bed.

"It wasn't an accident." He laughed again, and his gray eyes met mine for a moment before he studied the speckled tile floor. *"I was pissed. We just moved here from Boston, and I had to leave all my friends behind. It was stupid."*

"I ran away." My voice was barely a whisper, and I braced for him to ask me to elaborate, but he only nodded, his hand falling on my knee and giving it a small squeeze.

"It's not that bad here. I promise."

"Can't be any worse than home." I sighed dramatically.

"You're kind of intense, Lie." His lips quirked up in a smile, revealing deep dimples that settled into his cheeks, and I fought against a grin.

"So what are you? Like, the welcome committee or something?" I joked nervously as I pulled my lower lip between my teeth.

"You just looked like you needed a friend."

"Where were you a few years ago?" I rolled my eyes again, this time wishing I could pull out of my funk for five minutes. This guy was making an effort, and I probably was scaring him away.

"Well, I have plenty of time to make it up to you." There was no hint of humor in his expression, and I relaxed next to him.

"What did you think of Brock when you first met him?" Marie asked, shaking me from my memories, and I realized I was smiling.

"He was different. No one had ever really been nice to me before."

"So you liked him?"

"I don't know."

"Do you feel guilty for liking him?"

"Wouldn't you?" I sighed loudly as I ran my hand through my ponytail. "Look at what happened. If Brock never had met me he—"

Marie held up her hand to stop me from completing my thought. "We can't control other people's actions. You're only responsible for what *you* do. Do you think you did something wrong?"

"I existed." Unable to look her in the eye, I brushed away a tear that fell from my lashes.

"You aren't responsible for other people's actions. That includes your mother and Brock."

"It's not just what he did. I just…"

"You don't regret being with him." Marie finished my thought with a sigh. I nodded, not wanting to admit it out loud. "That's understandable, Delilah. You'd gone through a lot with the bullying and the issues with your mother. No one blames you for clinging to the one person who showed you kindness."

"Brock wasn't just kind. He was *everything*. He listened and he cared. He was protective of me, and for the first time in my life, I felt safe."

"Tell me about how he made you feel safe."

I readjusted in my seat as I looked at the drops on the window that had run together, blurring the picture of the outside world.

I was writing in my notebook, stuck on where I wanted my story to go. It's hard to even imagine a fictional happy ending when you've never experienced one in real life. A shadow fell over me as I lay on my stomach in bed, and I glanced up to see Brock smiling down at me. My heart instantly fluttered as I locked eyes with his. I tried to tell myself that the nervous feeling that settled in my stomach when he was near was from his intense personality. Brock was the kind of guy who could cut someone down with a glare, but his eyes softened when he looked at me, and I knew fear wasn't the cause of my nervousness.

"You gonna stay locked up in here like some Disney princess, or you gonna join the group?"

I dropped my pen on the paper as I let my eyes drift lower, roaming over his T-shirt, which read, "Anarchy" across his muscular chest.

"You like that?" He smirked, and I glanced up in time to catch him winking at me.

"What?" I pushed myself up from the bed and brushed my hair from my face.

"The shirt. It's one of my favorites."

"Yeah. It's cool." God, I was a bumbling idiot, but at least he thought I was checking out his dumb shirt and not his body.

"Some of the guys are about to play poker, and I think the girls are breaking out the board games. I need you to help me cheat." His dimples deepened in his cheeks as he grinned mischievously.

"I'm not going to help you cheat." I slid off my bed and slipped on my Chuck Taylors, not bothering to tie them.

"I need a partner in crime," he said.

"You need to stay out of trouble so you don't end up in places like this." I walked by him and into the hall, not wanting to be in there alone with him and risk getting in trouble.

"Last time I checked, you were locked up in this shithole too. That's like the spoon calling itself a plate."

I laughed so loudly that I had to cover my mouth with my hand, earning me a glare from one of the workers. "That's not how the saying goes."

"Then how does it go?" His hand nudged my side, and fire erupted in my veins, and it was all I could do to keep my knees from buckling. "The pot calling the kettle black. They're both black, so it means someone is being a hypocrite."

"Smart and beautiful. What's not to love about you?" Brock winked again, and his arm looped over my shoulders casually.

"Brock Ryan!" a stern voice called from behind us.

Brock glanced over his shoulder between us and chuckled as he removed his arm and put some distance between us. "You're gonna get me in trouble, Bird."

"You're the troublemaker, and my name is 'Lie.'"

"I like 'Bird.' It suits you."

My cheeks heated under his gaze, and I stared at the tiled floor, hoping he couldn't see me blush. We stopped at the entrance to the main lounge as he glanced around.

"What's your poison? You a card shark? You good at skimming off the top in Monopoly?" he joked.

"Actually I don't play a lot of games. You kind of have to have friends to play with."

"You got me, Bird." His arm went back around my shoulders, and I tried to shrug him off but didn't give it much effort. It was nice to have someone want to touch me. "Now pick something. I'll teach you."

"You'll cheat." I rolled my eyes and crossed my arms over my chest.

"I'd never cheat with you, Lie. I promise. I'm a man of my word. Now pick a game before I pick for us."

"Truth or dare."

Brock's jaw went slack, and his eyes widened slightly. "Oh…you have no idea how much fun this is going to be."

"I'll go first," I told him. "Truth or dare?"

His eyes drifted over my body, and I tightened my arms over my chest, feeling exposed under his gaze. "I'll go easy on you, Bird. Truth."

"Why are you being so nice to me?"

He shrugged. "Why not?"

"Because no one is nice to me. What do you want?" I tried to sound like I didn't care, but inside I was praying he wouldn't hurt my feelings.

"I just want to get to know you."

"Why?

"Why not?" he shot back, and I tried not to let my frustration get the best of me.

"Stop answering all my questions with questions. That's not how you play the game."

"I thought you didn't know how to play any games."

"Never mind." I dropped my arms and turned away from him so I could go back to my room and be alone, but his fingers wrapped around my upper arm and stopped me in my tracks. I refused to turn around and face him because my sadness was lurking just below the surface, and I already felt like a fool. Seeing it reflected in his eyes would be too much.

"When I first saw you, you looked so sad."

"That's not your problem," I snapped, and his hand fell from my arm.

"I know." His hands ran over his hair as I turned back to face him. "Look, you remind me of someone I miss very much. She always looked so sad, and if someone had taken the time to see what was wrong…" His voice trailed off.

"Oh, I get it. I'm some wounded animal you think needs to be taken care of." I didn't mean to lose my temper, but it hurt to know I was developing a crush on this guy, and he saw me as a poor little victim.

"No, Bird." He sighed and swallowed hard as he realized his nickname for me helped prove my point. "No, Lie. I don't see you as someone who needs to be taken care of. I'm just trying to be your friend."

As much as I could use a friend, I wanted Brock to be something more, and I knew now how stupid that was. God, I must have looked like such a pathetic little girl to him. "Helping me isn't going *to fix whoever it was that you didn't help from your past. So stop wasting our time. I don't need or want your help." I turned back toward my room and walked under shaky legs. I had to force myself not to run and make a complete fool out of myself.*

As I entered my room, I threw myself onto my bed, knocking my notebook to the floor. I buried my face in my sterile white blanket and let all my frustration pour from my eyes. For the first time, I wanted to be home, in my own room.

There was a knock on the open door, and I sniffled, wiping my eyes. "It's open, you jackass." I rolled over and looked at Brock through teary eyes. His hands were shoved into his jeans pockets, and he looked like he was contemplating coming farther into the room or just leaving me alone. Unfortunately my stupid teenage hormones were begging for him to come closer.

"I'm not using you to right some wrong, Lie." He stepped closer and looked at me to see if I was going to object. I put my chin on my hands and stared at the wall in front of me. "Laurie, my big sister, was two years into college. She was always a bubbly, over-the-top chick." He laughed at the memory and stepped closer. "My father— he hated me. I was never fast enough, never got the right position on the football team. He loved to hunt. Didn't matter what it was—he liked to kill. He was so proud of that gun collection of his. He used to beg me to go on trips with him, but my mom was always scared we'd end up killing each other because of how much we fought. But Laurie was perfect. She was a cheerleader and on the debate team. Man, she could argue." He laughed again, and I rolled onto my side and looked up at him. He was next to my bed now, and his eyes looked glazed over.

"Well, it must be a family trait. You're not so bad at arguing yourself," I teased, and was thankful when he gave me a half smile. I patted the bed, and he nodded as he sat down and turned to face me.

"When she left for college, it was like she sucked all the happiness out of the house."

I sat up and pulled my knees to my chest, resting my back against the wall. "So what happened? You're talking about her like she—"

"She died. Yeah…" He cleared his throat, and a single tear rolled down his cheek. I wanted to reach out and wipe it away, but I didn't move. "She loved college. She was popular, just like in high school. She was always calling me from parties and telling me how much I was going to love it when I went there."

"You planned to go to college?"

"I did. That was before." Brock shook his head and looked down at his hands. "I worked my ass off to get good grades. You wouldn't have believed it if you saw me."

"What happened?"

"One night Laurie called me. She was at some frat house but was sober; she was the designated driver. I blew her off. I was pissed about a fight Dad and I had gotten into. She was the person I always talked to about Dad. No one else really knew what kind of guy he was, but I didn't want to ruin her night. She said she'd call me in the morning to make sure I was OK." His eyes met mine, and I wasn't sure he was going to finish. I slid to the edge of the bed next to him, letting my legs dangle over the edge. "So the next day she didn't call, and I tried her cell a million times, but she wasn't answering."

"You can tell me." I placed my hand on his arm as he took a deep breath.

"She was in a car accident after she left the party. They said they tried to revive her, but she didn't respond."

"I'm so sorry, Brock."

"They found drugs in her system. My sister barely ever had a wine cooler, let alone touched drugs. She wouldn't have. Someone had to have slipped her something."

"Did they try to find out who it might have been?"

He shook his head and looked off at the open door. "They didn't believe us."

"I'm sorry about earlier. I had no idea."

"I know you didn't." He put his hand over mine and smiled sadly. "I don't want to be your friend because I think it'll somehow change my past. After Laurie died I stopped caring about anything, including myself. When I saw you sitting there looking so sad and alone, I realized you'd given up too. I saw it in those big brown eyes of yours." He lifted his hand and ghosted the pad of his thumb under my eye and slipped it into my messy long hair. "For the first time in a long while, I cared about something. I wanted to make you smile."

I grinned at his confession as his fingers tangled into my hair.

"I don't want to fix you, Bird. I want you to fix me."

I sucked in a ragged breath as his face slowly moved closer. His forehead pressed against mine as his strong arms wrapped around me, and he hugged me as if I were the last breath of air and he were struggling to keep his head above water. My arms slipped around his sides, and my eyes fell closed as his body shook and he cried silently into my neck. His hot tears slid over my collarbone as I ran my hands over the muscles of his back, trying to soothe him.

"You really do suck at games, Bird. Next time I'm picking."

I laughed as his arms squeezed me even tighter, making it difficult for me to breathe, but I didn't care as long as he didn't let me go.

"How did it feel, hearing about his past?" Marie asked, and my gaze snapped back to her, sadness weighing heavily on my chest.

"It broke my heart. Brock came off as this tough guy. I had no idea."

"You think because he was tough that he didn't experience pain?"

I shrugged, not wanting to think about Brock anymore, but I knew Marie wasn't done.

"You can be rather sarcastic," she continued. "Do you think you use that to keep people at arm's length?"

"I guess."

"Is that because of what you've been through?"

"You tell me. You're the one sitting on that side of the table." I rolled my eyes, and Marie sat back in her seat.

"Brock was the same way," she said. "He used intimidation to keep people out. You have a lot in common with him. It makes sense that the two of you would be drawn to each other."

"Moth to a flame. Somehow we both got burnt."

"You did great today, Delilah. This is the most you've shared with me about your past. You're making progress."

"It doesn't feel that way. It doesn't feel good to talk about it."

"It'll get easier. That's the point. One day at a time."

I gave Marie a weak smile as I pushed myself up from my seat and made my way to the door. My hand was on the knob as I looked over my shoulder at her. "You should consider some fake plants." I nodded to the sad pink flower on the sill that strangely now appeared wilted and dead. Perhaps I'd been here longer than I'd thought.

Maria laughed as her head shook slightly. "I'm not very good with living things. Better a flower than a house cat," she joked.

"Thank you," I said. I knew I didn't make it easy on Marie, but her taking the time to listen to me really did help.

She smiled back at me, and I left, needing to get as far away from this place, the truth, as possible.

Chapter Two

Escape

I managed to make it to my psych class today, but my mind was so focused on the session with Marie that I didn't absorb anything the professor said. As I sat around waiting for Trish to make it back to our apartment, I grabbed my cell phone and called my uncle, who I'd lived with when I'd first left Mississippi.

"You never call anymore. I thought you forgot my number," Uncle Greg joked, but his laugh turned into a hacking cough. I pictured his overgrown salt-and-pepper hair, his body doubled over as he struggled for breath. He was a good fifty pounds heavier than he'd been when I was a child.

"I've been busy." I sighed audibly as I dug through my closet for a shoebox I kept hidden away with keepsakes from high school.

"You know I worry about you, Delilah."

"I know. I'm sorry. I'm really liking college." My tone was positive as I found the box and pulled it onto my lap. I flipped off the lid, and my fingers ran over a photograph of Brock from the shelter.

"I'm glad. You deserve to be happy. You've been through a lot this past year. No one would blame you if you took a year off."

"Everyone blames me for everything." My teeth dug into my bottom lip as I looked at Brock and me together. We were so happy.

"That's not true," Uncle Greg said.

"I want to go see him," I said quietly, as I stared down at Brock's face.

"That's not a good idea, Delilah. He told you not to come back. You said yourself that Florida was a new start for you."

I heard the front door to our apartment open and close, and I knew Trish finally had returned. I put the lid back on the box and quickly hid it under a pile of clothes.

"I know. I'm sorry…I have to go. My roommate just got home, and we're going out tonight."

"Be safe."

"Always," I replied, as I hung up my cell and made my way into the living room. Trish's eyes met mine, and she smiled as she dropped her bag onto the couch.

"You ready?" she asked, as her eyes looked me over. I had changed into a jean skirt to show off my long legs but kept my tank top on. I wasn't much for getting all dressed up.

"Yeah, I just need to grab my purse."

"I'm going to change, and then we can get some food on our way to the party. Don't want to be seen eating like a pig in front of all the hot guys." She smirked as she wandered off to her room. I groaned but didn't make a comment. This was the world I'd chosen to throw myself into, and I'd never be accepted if I fought Trish on everything.

She was ready to go in only ten minutes and looking like she'd just stepped off the cover of a slutty magazine. I hated how effortless it was for Trish to be beautiful. Her long blond curls seemed to move around her like she always had her face in the wind.

"How do I look?" she asked, her perfect white smile spread from ear to ear.

"Like a slut," I joked, and she smacked my arm. "I'm kidding. You know you're beautiful."

Her smile changed, and it looked more genuine, not like the cookie-cutter Barbie doll I was used to. "Ian loved it when I wore this skirt."

I glanced down at her short, black, pleather skirt that barely concealed her underwear. I gave her a hard look as I pulled open the front door and let her walk out before me.

"Don't look at me that way, Lie. As soon as I'm out of college, he and I are getting a place together."

"He's your stepfather, and last I checked, paying someone off to keep them a secret isn't exactly a declaration of love."

"How would you know, virgin?"

"I'm not a virgin." I rolled my eyes as we made our way to Trish's black 300S parked along the busy street.

"Oh, right. I forgot about your precious Brock," she joked, as she smiled over the roof of her car. I opened the passenger door and slid in, ready to call this whole thing off.

"Brock is a completely different situation." I tried to hide the anger in my voice. Trish didn't know about my past. I knew I looked like a love-sick puppy to her.

"I know. I'm sorry."

Trish pushed the button on the dash to start the car, and we pulled out into traffic as she sighed loudly, her brow furrowed.

"What?" I asked her.

"I just wish you'd open up to me more. I told you about Ian. That's not exactly something to be proud of—I know. Anyway, I'm here for you."

I'd like to think that a friend offering to listen to my problems wasn't shocking, but Trish was as deep as a frying pan. I knew, under all that mascara and bleach, that she cared, but she never let that side of her slip out. I envied the way she could lock her real self away from others.

"Besides, you know how I love to gossip." She actually giggled. My faith in humanity was lost again.

I never expected a deep, meaningful friendship with Trish. In fact I loved her for her lack of empathy. I didn't want anyone to care, to ask me too many questions. I wanted to start my life over and become a new person.

We drove through Orlando and sat in traffic until the sun sank below the hotels as I let my mind wander to the past.

I picked at the tattered shoelace of my white Chucks, wishing I knew how long my mother was going to keep me locked in this dump. It was a joke. They treated us like prison inmates, and just three floors below was a YMCA. Did the people down there know that dozens of teenagers were being held against their will right above them? The boys were housed on the third floor, but they came up to the fourth with the girls to eat, learn, and hang out throughout the day.

"Keep looking sad, and they'll take those shoes from you," a thick, familiar accent called from above me. I glanced up to see Brock standing over me, his lips turned up in a grin.

"Why would they take my shoes? Can't they let me have anything that distracts me?"

"They'll think you're a runner, and I'm here to distract you." He winked as he sat next to me, his back pressed against the pea-green

wall, and nodded across the room. "See that douche bag over on the couch with the fucked-up hair? They took his shoes the day I got here. Said he shoved one of the guys who guards the door and threatened to burn this place down."

"How would he burn it down?" I asked, as my eyes scanned the lanky boy who sat quietly by himself across the room.

Brock shrugged as he brought his knees up and rested his arms across them. "Fuck if I know. This place doesn't matter anyway."

"Do you know when they'll let you out?"

He turned to look me in the eye, the playful smirk gone and no hint of humor in his voice. "This is much better than what's waiting for me out there, and they say it's up to our parents. How fucked up is that? My dad would let me live here until I turned eighteen if he could."

"Better than being in school." I focused on my shoes again, and Brock was quiet beside me for a moment. "What about your mom?"

He shook his head, and the muscles in his jaw jumped as he clenched it tightly. "She does whatever Dad says. Kind of how it works in my house. You go to Natchez High?"

I nodded as I glanced up at one of the workers, who was watching me play with my shoe. I dropped the lace and pulled my legs underneath me.

"Good. It'll be nice to know someone when I start."

For the first time since I could remember, I was looking forward to going to school, and I beamed at the thought.

"So why don't you like school?" Brock asked me.

"Does anyone actually like school?" I retorted, but I knew he wasn't going to drop it. He had opened up to me, and now it was my turn.

"Nah, I guess you're right." He laughed and shook his head. "I always skipped."

"I wish I could, but it's nice to have a meal in the middle of the day."

"You call that food? I should cook for you sometime. I make a mean spaghetti."

"You're kidding? You cook?" I made all my food for myself, but we never had anything that wasn't microwavable.

Brock shrugged. "Not really, but I can teach you how to make spaghetti." We both laughed, and my shoulder bumped against him. "Everyone in here is pissed off at the world. It's nice to see you smile. Gives me hope."

"It's nice to be happy for once." I ran my teeth over my lower lip, and he used his thumb to pull it free.

"Careful. I'll tell one of the guys in charge that you're trying to hurt yourself. Now tell me why you hate school."

I sighed as I looked at all the throwaway kids who surrounded us. We'd all been tossed aside for one reason or another. We all struggled to find a place. But it wasn't so bad here, especially with Brock by my side. "People kind of hate me there."

"You?" he said with genuine shock in his voice.

"Yes. Me. I've never cared about being one of the cool kids, and I've always been miserable at home, so of course I'm a ball of sunshine at school. When I we hit middle school, all the girls were curling their hair and starting to use makeup."

"Makeup?" He shook his head. "I'll never understand why girls like to spread that dirt on their faces." I glared at him, and he held his hands in the air in mock surrender. "Continue," he said with a laugh.

"As I was saying, all the girls were starting to wear makeup, and my mom never really cared about that kind of stuff when it came to me. She didn't teach me how to use it and all that fun stuff."

"So what did you do?"

I glanced at Brock, who looked genuinely interested in my story. "I stole her makeup bag one morning before school and flipped through a magazine to try to figure out how to use it. I thought I did pretty well." I laughed at how stupid I'd been. "I went to school with my head held high. I thought for sure the other girls would look at me like I was one of them. But instead…" I cleared my throat as I picked at my shoe. "Instead they laughed at me. Said I was practicing to be a whore like my mother."

"Why did they think that about your mom?" he asked, as I tried to wipe away my tears discreetly.

"Because my mom was raped at fifteen by a family friend. She didn't want to have me, but my grandparents shamed her into keeping me. She used to try to come to school events and parent conferences, but the other parents made her feel like she didn't belong because she was so much younger than them. So she eventually stopped trying."

"Jesus…"

"It was better that she stopped coming, but the damage was done. The parents talked, and it didn't take long for the kids to start talking too. Even though my mom never really cared, I tried to stand up for her, but that made everyone hate me more." The tears flowed freely now, and I didn't bother to wipe them away. "So…the makeup was a disaster, and by the end of the day, I looked like a raccoon from crying off my mascara and eyeliner. That was the last day I tried, and everything got much worse."

"Those days are over, Bird. Now we have each other, and I won't let them make you cry anymore."

"You promise?" I asked, as Brock used the palm of his hand to brush the sadness from my cheeks.

"I promise."

"Fucking tourists!" Trish ran her hand through her hair angrily.

"We can't all be born and raised in sunny Florida." I reached out and turned up the radio as the car inched toward our exit.

The party would have long been swinging, and I was thankful. I wasn't a people person, but the new Lie liked to go out and have fun. The new Lie loved to dance and party and give the world hell.

We pulled up in front of an older house I was sure would have passed for a mansion back when it was built. It had since become run-down, separated into apartments then converted back to a single-family home. I gave Trish an unsure look, but she grabbed my wrist and pulled me toward the door as she pushed the alarm button on her key chain.

The sun had disappeared, and in the moonlight, the building looked like a haunted house surrounded by woods. The steps to the front door actually creaked under the weight of our bodies. Trish didn't bother knocking; she just pushed open the door. I expected loud music and bodies everywhere, but the music was faint, and I vaguely heard people's voices. That's when I realized there were only a few cars outside.

I stopped walking, and Trish turned around to glare at me. "Don't be such a baby. It's fine. This is an exclusive gathering." The corner of her pouty pink lips turned up in a smirk. I shook my head but let her pull me farther inside.

The house wasn't as run-down as I'd thought, but it definitely could stand a new coat of pain and a heavy cleaning.

"In here," a deep voice called out, and we walked through the entryway into the living room.

The walls were a deep olive, and there were two matching green couches along the walls.

"We're ready to party." Trish released my hand as she walked over to one of the couches and sat between two college-age guys. One leaned back and put his arm behind her then stretched out his long legs. I glanced at the love seat, which had only one guy sitting on it. My heart sped up double time as I took in his dirty-blond hair and light stubble over his jaw. He patted the cushion next to him, and I reluctantly walked over and took a seat alongside him, careful to keep my leg from touching his.

I recognized one of the guys who sat next to Trish; he was in my lit class. His name was Adam, and he was built like a football player, his hair dark and thick but cut short. The boy who had his arm around Trish was a stranger to me, as was the guy I sat next to.

"I won't bite," the guy next to me said, and I realized I was practically clinging to the arm of the love seat to keep my distance. I relaxed back in my seat, but I didn't feel comfortable in this situation.

"So you got us in your rape den. Where's the goods?" Trish obviously wasn't worried about these guys.

Adam chuckled as he leaned back and dug into his jeans pocket. He pulled out a small medicine bottle, unscrewed the child-safety cap, and dumped the contents into his hand. Trish eagerly held out her palm, with an anxious grin plastered on her plastic face. I wished I were back at our apartment. I'd only known her about a year, and she'd gotten me into more sticky situations than I could count—the worst of which being the time she'd passed out in the middle of the library, and I had to lie to a teacher's aide to help me get her to her car. I was rewarded by Trish vomiting on me in front of everyone. The good thing about Trish was that she didn't care about my past—who I was or why I needed to be someone else. All she cared about was herself, which was both sad and relieving. Picking at my thumbnail, I sank back into my seat as guy number one fed his drugs to Trish and the other two guys as if they were baby birds.

The guy next to me reached to the small stand beside the love seat and grabbed a mint tin. The back of his hand bumped my leg, and he motioned with his chin for me to follow him. I was the dumb blonde in every scary movie I'd ever seen, but I stood from the couch and followed him around the corner and up a flight of stairs.

"You didn't look like you wanted to party," he said, as he glanced over his shoulder. His teeth flashed brilliantly white against his sun-kissed skin. No killer could be that beautiful, so I followed. Some people never learn.

"Not really my scene," I mumbled, as we made our way into a small empty room. I immediately went to the window, where the moonlight poured in.

"Mine either."

"Then why are you here?" I turned back to look at him. He leaned against the wall as he pulled something out of the tin and dug around in his pocket.

"Why are *you* here?" he asked, as he put a joint between his lips and held the lighter to the end. It glowed hot orange, and shadows danced against his skin.

"Nowhere else to be."

He nodded as if he understood as smoke drifted from around his lips. It was mesmerizing. He held the joint out to me, and I stepped closer to him and took it between my fingers as he exhaled, engulfing me in a white cloud.

"We traded one drug for another?" I raised an eyebrow, and he grinned, his eyelids heavy.

"Pot isn't a drug." He chuckled as he ran his fingers through his messy, dirty-blond hair.

"What is this place?" I asked, as I held the joint to my lips and inhaled, filling my lungs.

"It's nowhere." His reddening eyes locked on mine as he threw my words back at me. I grinned as I let the smoke expel from my lungs and instantly felt lighter.

"It looks like it's ready to fall apart." I held the joint out, and his fingers ran over mine as he took it, sending a shiver down my spine.

"Nah." He glanced around the room. "It just needs some love."

My cheeks began to burn as he studied my face, and I squirmed under his gaze. "It's a house that everyone has forgotten about," I told him.

"It was once someone's home. It was a dream, a future." He took another drag as he stared down at the glowing cherry. "And it hasn't been forgotten. Not yet. We're here."

"We're here and nowhere."

"Exactly." He pointed at me and nodded.

"I think you're high." I laughed as I took another hit, shaking my head. It wasn't often I was able to let the stress slip away. I felt brand new. The past fell away to the present with no thoughts given to the future. I was high. I backed up against a wall and slid down, my knees against my chest.

"I'm Abel Jensen," he said, as he slid down against the wall next to me, his head resting against its peeling surface.

"Lie," I said, as he smirked.

"It really is," he said, his eyes narrowing.

I laughed, loud and bubbly. "I believe you. I'm Delilah Monroe, 'Lie' for short."

He chuckled as he ran his palms over the front of his cargo shorts. He wore a plain white T-shirt that hugged his long, lean muscles.

"You surf?" I asked, as I studied him. He looked carefree and easygoing, but his eyes looked tired, and not just from the pot.

"Not as much as I used to."

"You live so close to the beach. I get it, though. Classes kind of take up all my time too."

"I never go." His eyes flicked up to mine and back to his shorts. He looked embarrassed.

"Why not?" I crossed my legs and rested my elbows on the insides of my thighs.

He shrugged but didn't answer. I leaned back against the wall and ran my hand through my long blond hair, grabbing a chunk and holding it in front of my eyes as I inspected the split ends from the constant dye jobs.

"The waves in Cali are so much better." The easygoing smile was back on his lips, and I couldn't look away. "You ever been?"

"No." I leaned forward, my arm extended for him to take the joint back. "I'm done," I said, as he took it from me and held it to his perfect mouth. I got lost in the thought that I'd just had my lips on it, and it felt like we'd done something intimate.

"It's beautiful," he said, as he shook his head slightly, like he was in on a joke that I had missed.

"I'm sure it is." I sighed as I stretched my legs and silently cursed Trish for letting me wear a skirt.

"I meant your hair." His eyes studied me, and I watched them dip lower, running the length of my bare legs before he met my eyes again. "Reminds me of that actress in *Garden State*."

"Thanks. Wait…wasn't she a brunet?" My body felt hot, and I knew I was pink all over as I cocked my head to the side, but

Abel just shook his head as his high settled in. I wasn't used to boys hitting on me. High school had been pure hell for me—besides Brock. My chest ached and tightened as he ran through my mind. A lot had changed since Mississippi. Brock was too far away. Even being in front of him would feel like a million miles away. I was no longer the sad, worthless girl who cowered and cried to herself. I was no one, anyone, and anything I wanted to be.

"What?" I asked, as I realized his eyes were still on me.

"Nothing." Abel shrugged as he let the joint burn out and placed it back in the mint tin.

"I should probably get going." I pushed up from the floor, careful not to flash my panties. I really did want to kick Trish's ass for not telling me where we were really going.

"Your friend is probably going to need you to take care of her for a while." He stood and stretched, his cotton T-shirt lifting to reveal the hard ridges of his abs.

"What did she take?" I asked, as I ran my hands over the back of my skirt.

"X." He shook his head as he clenched his jaw, the muscles pulling and flexing under his skin.

"She's an idiot." I shook my head as well but immediately regretted my words. Trish was supposed to be my friend, but sometimes I couldn't stand her.

Abel laughed as he rubbed his palm over the back of his neck. "She's in good company then."

I glanced up to his blue-green-ocean eyes, and he winked, setting free a thousand butterflies in my stomach. I realized my mouth was hanging open, and I snapped my lips together as I nervously tucked my hair behind my ear and made my way from the room. Abel followed me down the creaky stairs, and I suddenly felt like pushing open the front door and taking off into the night. So that's what I did. As my foot came off the bottom step, I pushed forward and grabbed the door handle, but it didn't turn, and my paranoia from my high began to creep over me. I turned around to face Abel, whose eyebrows were pulled together as I pressed my back against the door. He kept coming, his body so close that I felt the heat from his skin, and goose bumps broke out over my arms as he reached out and twisted the lock on the handle. I breathed out, realizing I'd been holding it in, and the corner of his lip twitched upward as he took a small step back.

I spun around and pulled the door open, my lungs desperate for fresh air. I walked out into the night, down the steps of the porch, and put my hands on my knees as I gasped.

"Are you all right?" Abel called from behind me. I shook my head, not wanting to hear my voice sound weak. Nothing could make me look any more pathetic than my panic attack. Fear crept up from my stomach and spread through my body. *There's nothing to be scared of,* I repeated over and over in my head. A hand spread out over my back, and I shot up and turned to see Abel with concern in his eyes, hidden behind the red glaze. The color made the swirling sea color pop, and I stared, mesmerized. He wasn't trying to hurt me. No one was trying to hurt me anymore, but it didn't stop the fear that raced in my chest and made me feel as if my heart would explode.

"I just need…a minute." I looked down at the gravel and grass, which were illuminated by the moonlight.

"Just breathe, Delilah." His hand was on my back again, and he slowly counted down from ten, his voice low and soothing. I couldn't help get lost in it and let it cloud my thoughts.

"You a shrink or something?" I joked, as I finally started to come back around.

"No, but I've seen my fair share."

"So you're crazy. Good to know."

"Just needed someone to talk to," he said.

I got that. I got it more than Abel realized. I didn't know what I'd do without Marie, but there were things I couldn't even tell her. It was like a brick resting on my chest, on my conscience. It weighed a ton, and I would have loved to have someone help me carry it, take some of the pressure off me, but Brock was out of reach. I could picture him right then, and it made my heart hum.

"Good morning." Brock stuck his head inside my room, and I jumped from my bed.

"You'll get in trouble if they catch you in here."

Brock stepped farther into my room and crossed his arms over his chest, a playful smirk on his lips. "Do you want me to leave?"

I bit my lip as I stared at him. I shook my head, and he smiled at me.

"Then I'm not leaving."

"They'll make you. They'll take away your privileges." I stepped closer to him and lowered my voice so no one would hear.

"It'll be worth it, Bird."

My heart raced at his nickname for me, and for the millionth time, I wanted to ask him what it meant, but my heart was stuck in my throat, and that was when I noticed a sadness in his eyes.

"What's wrong?" I asked him.

"Nothing." He laughed nervously and shook his head.

"Seriously? You have to tell me, or I'm going to scream."

His eyebrow cocked as if he were challenging me. I opened my mouth, but before the sound left my throat, Brock's body was flush against mine, his strong hand over my mouth as he smiled.

"You trying to get me in trouble, Bird? That's not very nice. I thought we were friends."

*I tried to ignore the fact that he had called me his friend.
It boggled my mind that he'd risk getting into trouble just to be
near me—not that I was complaining. His hand slid from my
mouth, and I sucked in a ragged breath, suddenly very aware of
his hard, muscular body, which was pressed against mine. His eyes
narrowed, and the smirk fell from his lips as we studied each other.*

*"Want to know why I'm sad?" he said. "My mom called this
morning to let me know my grandma died. She isn't even getting me
out to go to her funeral back in Boston." His arm fell from my waist,
and I wobbled on my feet as my emotions went from one extreme to
the next along with Brock's. My heart was racing from his nearness
and breaking over his pain.*

*"I'm sorry." I had no idea what to say. I'd never had a friend, let
alone had to comfort one while he or she was hurting.*

*"Nothing to be sorry about, Bird." He shrugged, the sad gaze
now carefully masked behind a blank stare. "Shit happens, right?"
he spat angrily.*

I nodded as I picked at my thumbnail.

*"Hey." He stepped closer, the palm of his hand sliding over my
cheek, and I struggled not to lean into his touch. "I'm fine. I'm sorry.
I shouldn't have dumped that on you. This isn't your problem." He
stepped back, his hand falling to his side as he turned to leave the
room.*

*"Wait," I whisper-yelled after him as he stepped into the hall.
"Wait for me." I followed after him, and his lips formed a smile.*

"Always, Bird."

"Where did you go just now?" Abel was in front of me,
his face full of concern. I felt like a fool, getting lost in my
memories.

"I just spaced out." I forced a laugh. "I must really be high."

He smiled back, but it didn't reach his eyes. He looked worried. I walked toward the house. Maybe if I hung out with Trish, I could stop thinking about my problems. Abel walked with me, but he stayed a step behind.

"Trish?" I called out as I stepped inside. I walked into the living room, and Trish was on one of the guys' laps as she kissed him fiercely, her hips rocking to the beat of whatever song was playing. She was still fully clothed, but something told me it wouldn't be long until that changed. Douche bag number two was watching them intently, his hand down the front of his jeans. "Trish!"

She pulled back from the guy's face but kept her hands on his cheeks as she turned to look at me. Her smile grew wide, and I took a step back.

"You wanna join?" Her high-pitched laugh turned my stomach, and I shook my head as I spun around, nearly running into Abel. "I knew you weren't completely worthless."

"It's the drugs. Just ignore her," he whispered, but I even as I tried to feel anger instead of sadness, tears filled my eyes. It was an odd relief for the dryness of my high, and I wanted to let everything out but not in front of this guy. I refused to look like any more of a fucking loser. I didn't need to do anything, though; Trish took care of that for me. It was high school all over again.

"Whatever. It's not like Brock would care anyway. He never even calls you." She made a snorting sound as she laughed, and I found it fitting that she sounded like a pig as she made fun of me. The guys on the couch didn't seem to care about the ugliness she spewed, because she was pretty on the outside, and that's all that ever mattered.

I pushed by Abel and stopped in front of the door. I couldn't just leave her there. I wasn't that kind of person. Instead I turned toward the other archway and walked into a small kitchen.

My eyes fixed on a tan piece of trim that looked severely out of place in the dilapidated house. I glanced at the refrigerator, and my stomach growled.

"Hungry?" Abel's voice was hushed, and the smell of weed and his cologne filled the musky room. I nodded, feeling like a fool for not leaving.

He walked around me and pulled open a cupboard. Inside was a plastic grocery bag full of goodies. He placed it on the island and smiled as he looked at me.

"Always be prepared." He pulled out a box of cookies and a bag of chips.

"You're a Boy Scout. I think I liked you better when I thought you were crazy," I joked, and he laughed, shaking his head.

"I never said I *wasn't* crazy." His eyebrows rose as he held up the cookies. I nodded, and he slid over to me as he pulled a small bottle from the bag. He twisted off the cap and popped a pill into his mouth.

"She's not normally like this." I didn't know why I felt the need to explain Trish to Abel.

"I know what she's like." He didn't elaborate, and my heart sank as I realized he probably knew Trish very well. Everyone did. He didn't seem the least bit fazed that she was preparing for a gang bang in the next room either.

I took a bite of a chocolate chip cookie, my eyes falling closed as I savored the deliciousness.

"Good, huh?" He grabbed one from the pack and popped the entire thing into his mouth.

"Why are you here?" I didn't intend for the question to sound rude, but my filter seemed to flicker on and off.

"Same reason you are."

"I didn't know this was where I was going, or I probably wouldn't have come."

"Well…" His eyes shimmered as the moonlight caught them. "I'm glad you didn't know." My heart thumped double time in my chest before he continued. "It can suck baby-sitting those assholes alone."

"I know the feeling." I rolled my eyes and finished my cookie as Trish called out from the other room and the music grew louder. "Help yourself to the snacks." He sat the bottle on the counter, and the pills rattled.

He smirked and left the kitchen to see what she wanted. Morbid curiosity wanted me to follow, but I took another cookie and waited, not wanting to be tormented by Trish.

Abel was a good guy, here for his friend, just like I was. I let my imagination drift as I pictured him lying on a surfboard, his hands dipping into water that matched the color of his eyes. He seemed like he had no cares whatsoever. I wondered why he'd ever need to see a shrink. It didn't make any sense. I picked up the pill bottle and read the label. He was on Vicodin now, and I knew I'd just become his baby-sitter as well. The giggling and cheers grew louder, and I grabbed a cookie as I walked past the stairs to the living room. Abel was on the love seat, where I'd seen him when I'd first come in. Now Trish was straddling his lap and dancing to "Boom" by Anjulie.

It clicked. In that second it made sense. Abel didn't seem like that type of guy because he was pretending, just like I was. He was a lie. Or maybe I wanted to see kindness in someone else because it was so rare in my life. Not that I could blame or judge him. I was no different. We were the same and so very, very different.

"Stop being a whore, and come play a game with us," Trish said.

"Wouldn't want to give you any competition." Hilarious choice of words coming from a girl who'd made out with three strangers tonight. They weren't strangers to her, though. I was the stranger. I was the one on the outside. My mind drifted back to truth or dare with Brock.

"What game?" I asked, hating myself for following the crowd, but what choice did I have? This was Lie, the popular girl. I wasn't a loser anymore and could prove it.

"Spin the bottle." Trish glanced over her shoulder and winked as Abel's hands slid over his hips.

"That's a kids' game."

Chapter Three

Stutter

"Have you ever even kissed a guy, Lie?" Trish was running her hands over Abel's chest.

"You kn-know I have," I replied quietly as Adam stepped closer to me and brushed my hair over my shoulder.

"I'll kiss you." He took another step, his hand gliding over his stomach and down over his jeans.

"You're gross," I snapped, and Abel laughed, loud and deep.

"Leave her the fuck alone, Adam. She's not interested in you." His eyes met mine, and it felt like something was implied by his statement, and it pissed me off. "She has a boyfriend," he said with a sarcastic smirk.

Thank you, Trish, for bringing up Brock. My insides boiled. I just wanted to escape my past for one damn night. Was that too much to ask?

"I'll play," I said, my voice coming out strong and confident. All part of the lie. I felt like an idiot for trying to fit in with these people.

"That's my girl!" Trish slid off Abel's lap, and he ran his hand along his strong jaw before sliding off the couch and sitting across from me. Adam was at my side, and Trish was on the other. The other guy was relaxing on the couch, his hand still in his pants as he stroked himself. I wanted to vomit.

I grabbed the empty vodka bottle from the floor and laid it on its side. I tried not to look at Abel as I spun it. It rotated endlessly, and I felt like an idiot for spinning it so hard. When it stopped I glanced up at green-blue eyes, and Abel smiled as I looked over at Trish, and my heart sank a little.

"Get over here, you little slut!" She pushed to her knees, nearly falling over as she scooted toward me. I swallowed hard as I met her halfway and pressed my lips against hers. Her gloss tasted like cherries and cigarettes. I tried to look unaffected as she slid the tip of her tongue over my bottom lip to elicit cheers from the guys.

"I knew you had it in you." Trish swiped her thumb below her lip to fix her makeup as she winked and sat back next to Abel.

Trish spun next, and the bottle landed on Adam. He smirked as his hands slid into her hair. Their kiss was loud and sloppy, and I blushed as I glanced at Abel. The air in the room was changing, charged with sexual tension.

Their hands roamed over each other's bodies, and I grew increasingly uncomfortable as they clawed at each other's clothing. Abel cleared his throat, and they broke apart.

"My turn," I said, and grabbed the bottle. I spun and tried my best to keep my gaze off the stormy ocean eyes across from me. As the neck slowed and stopped in front of Abel, my heart thudded against my chest like it was trying to break free. I rose to my knees, but Abel didn't move, and I was losing my nerve. "You could at least meet me halfway." I didn't mean to sound bitchy, but if he expected me to throw myself on him like Trish did with Adam, he was going to be disappointed. He just watched me. I was humiliated.

"Ugh. You're such a child," Trish groaned.

As I watched her leg slide over Abel's lap and her nails slide through his messy beach hair, I realized I'd never be her. I wasn't that good of a pretender. Her lips pressed hard against Abel's, and I felt my stomach turn. Why did everyone like her so much? What was so good about Trish Wentworth that I didn't have?

I got up from the circle and made my way into the kitchen. I vaguely heard Adam moan about not getting his chance with me, and I rolled my eyes as I stood in front of the kitchen island. This was supposed to be different, and I was being the same old Delilah. I grabbed the pill bottle and dumped a few in my hand before popping them into my mouth and dry-swallowing them. A pill lodged in my throat, and I dug around in the bag until my hands landed on a bottle of Gatorade. I chugged it down, freeing the pill from its spot.

I was a doormat on a bad day and a baby-sitter on the few good ones. Trish didn't view me as an equal, and I never saw her as being mine either. We used each other like everyone else on the planet, and I just took a while to see it. I grabbed the box of cookies and made my way to the front porch, where I sunk down on the old wooden steps and stared up at the moon. It wasn't quite full, but it was enormous.

I ate a cookie as I thought about Marie. I could see the disapproval in her face now as I told her all about this night. I couldn't tell her. I couldn't see that look from her. She was the only one I truly had, and even that was just means to an end.

I needed to get over Brock, or his memory would kill me. Marie was using me as well; I was a paycheck.

"You should see what the hell is going on in there." Abel stumbled out of the door laughing, a cigarette dangling from his lips as he sat beside me, using my knee as a brace so he wouldn't tumble down the rest of the stairs.

I glanced over at him, now shirtless. His skin seemed to glow under the moon, and my eyes focused on a thin white scar that ran over his ribs.

"I'd rather not," I said dryly as he lit his cigarette, inhaling deeply and groaning as he released the smoke.

"Yeah." He shook his head and laughed as he pulled another drag. "Probably too X-rated for a girl like you."

I didn't like the way he said "girl," like I was a fucking child. I grabbed his cigarette and took a drag, my eyes locked on his.

"You don't look like the type," he said, as he took it back and pressed it between his lips.

"Looks can be deceiving." I stared off into the night, the pills slowly starting to dull the anger that throbbed in the back of my head. I wobbled, unsteady, and leaned back on my arms. The cracked wood dug into my elbows, but I was too focused on the wave of euphoria that was slowly licking at my toes and weaving its way through my veins.

"Like this house. It looks like it's not worth shit, but there are memories here. Old ones." He looked at me again. "New ones. You have to look past the chipped paint and creaky floorboards, but it's there."

I nodded, but my mind was pulsing in waves, and I lay on my back, the splintery wood poking me through my shirt. Abel did the same, and we stared out at the moon as he pulled another drag from his cigarette. The night was quiet, just the sound of our deep breaths as we got lost in our own thoughts. He began to ramble, picking up where he'd left off, but his sentences ran together, and he never seemed to complete a thought.

"You can't change what's on the inside…inside people, not the house. The house can be changed." The cherry from his cigarette blew brighter as he took a long pull and exhaled slowly. "Not really true, though. I changed. Things changed. My whole life…" He tucked his arm under his head to angle his face toward the moon.

"I've changed but not really. Changed a lot in some ways, others not at all," I offered, but my words got caught on my tongue, and I stuttered as I tried to push out a thought. I felt deep, but the translation was lost on its way from my brain to my tongue. I felt like I was sinking into the old wood of the porch, becoming the decrepit house that had been forgotten.

"What are you on?" Abel was on his side, propped on his elbow and looming over me, blocking the light of the moon.

"A dilapidated porch," I replied with a smirk, as if I'd deciphered a trick question. His eyebrows pulled together, and I wanted to reach out and smooth the skin between them, but I was frozen under the stormy ocean of his eyes.

"Did you take some of those pills?" His body swayed slightly, or maybe my vision was impaired.

"Sorry." I shrugged and ran my hand over my face. My skin tingled and itched from the medication. I wanted to scratch it all away, peel the paint from my shell, and see whether what was inside was just as fucked up, but I knew it was.

"How many?" His voice was stern, and I felt like I was about to be lectured by my father, but I didn't have a father, so I wasn't sure whether I should laugh or cry.

"Two…maybe three." I fought the smile that tugged at the corner of my lips. The moonlight made him look like an angel with a glowing halo, and I wanted to run my hand through his hair to see if the magic would scatter around him and float off into the thick night air.

"Fuck," he mumbled as his jaw flexed. He was angry, but it seemed aimed at himself.

"I'm sorry." I felt sadness inside me, but the pills held it off, kept the tears from ever hitting the surface. I no longer wanted to feel. My thoughts became words, and I pushed myself up to sit too fast. "I don't belong here."

His long fingers wrapped around my arms, and he held me firmly in place. "Tonight you do."

My eyes focused on his lips, and the smell of cookies, toothpaste, and smoke blew over my face. My tongue ran over my lower lip, and I could taste the sin. It was thick and heavy in the air, and it made my head swim as I gazed into Abel's ocean-colored eyes. I wondered whether he tasted it too, whether his heart was pounding in his chest. I wondered most of all if it was artificial—a haze of adoration brought on by the pills. It had been so long since I'd wanted that; I didn't trust my own thoughts, but it felt too good to care.

"Do you want me to call your boyfriend?" His words broke the spell, and I looked up into the endless depths of his eyes and slowly shook my head. "Fuck. He's going to be pissed." He stood up and ran his hand through his hair, but I still felt the lingering tingle from his touch and the goose bumps that crept down my arms.

"He won't be," I said so quietly that I wasn't sure he could hear me, but he nodded once, and I swallowed hard. There was no boyfriend; he wasn't that anymore. He was the only one who ever cared, and now I couldn't see him, and it was all my fault. The heavy ache in my chest overpowered the high, and I want to scream; I wanted to break something.

"Then he's just as fucking stupid as I am." Abel tugged at his sandy-blond hair, and I smiled as I gazed his green-blue eyes. He was like a walking slice of summer.

I wanted to defend Brock, place the blame where it should be, but I couldn't. Doing so would mean explaining, and explaining wasn't how I coped. I coped with secrets and lies and fake smiles.

"He's in Mississippi." That was the only truth I could offer. He was there and I was here, and that was all anyone needed to know.

Abel sat back down next to me, his arms resting on his knees as he shook his head.

"I'm fine," I told him.

His eyes met mine, and he laughed but without humor. "You're trouble." His hand rubbed over my hair like I was a bratty little sister, and I sunk further into the numbness so I wouldn't have to wonder why that bothered me so much.

"I should check on Trish." I started to stand up, but Abel grabbed my hand and looped his fingers in mine then pulled me back down.

"You don't want to go in there. You'll be scarred for life."

"It's not like I haven't seen her fucking guys before." The bite in my words shocked me, but I was sick of being treated like her sidekick.

Abel laughed, deep and throaty, his body vibrating beside mine as he pulled his hand from mine. "You're *nothing* like her."

I don't know why his words offended me, because it was the truth. I was nothing like Trish.

"You don't even know me." I stood, and this time he didn't grab my hand. He just sat there, staring at the moon, as I disappeared inside.

Trish was pinned under Adam, her shirt pushed up and his removed. She was panting and moaning as the music made the thin walls vibrate.

The other guy ran his hands through his hair, his eyes closed, just feeling. It was an odd scene, and I wanted to look away, but I was curious. What made her so popular? Sure, I got more attention now than I ever did in high school, but it paled compared to her. I'd always be in that shadow.

Chapter Four

Liar, Liar

"You look good enough to eat," the guy on the couch slurred, and I realized he caught me staring at Trish and Adam. I swayed slightly, feeling tired but electrified.

He stood and walked slowly toward me, but it wasn't sexy. He reminded me of the killer in scary movies who stalks his prey, walking, plotting, always a step away.

"Gross," I mumbled, but my words didn't offend him. He took another step, and I looked down at Trish. She was oblivious to the somersaults inside my stomach. Even if she were remotely coherent, she probably would make fun of me as usual.

I took a step back and rocked on my heels as I bumped into a hard chest. I didn't need to turn around to know it was Abel. I smelled the smoky cologne all around me.

"Knock it off, Sean, or fucking leave."

Dirtbag Sean raised his hands like it was an honest mistake and backed up to the couch, falling back as his legs hit the edge.

"At least someone wants to kiss me," I mumbled angrily, the stab of rejection from Abel still in the forefront of my mind.

"Come on." Abel slipped his hand in mine and pulled me toward the stairs. I hesitated, pulling away as dizziness swirled my thoughts like a tornado. Abel slipped his hand under my knees and lifted me like a child as he ascended the stairs.

I closed my eyes, bathing in the touch of another person. It had been too long since I'd been hugged, held, or cared for.

We turned left at the top of the stairs and entered a room I hadn't seen. As he pushed the door open, I blinked, adjusting to the darkness. Abel walked a few steps inside and placed me on a mattress. I curled onto my side, and a blanket was draped over my legs. I heard the shuffle of his feet and the squeak of the door closing, and I was alone.

I don't know how long I was able to hold my eyes open, but eventually sleep won out, and I drifted into twisted nightmares and sad memories. The banging sound inside my skull was as real as hearing it with my own ears, and I sat up, soaked in sweat, my throat raw, and worried I may have screamed in real life. The door shoved open, and I saw the silhouette of Abel, wearing only boxer briefs.

"Are you OK?" His voice was throaty and harsh from the night of partying. His eyes darted around the room, and he relaxed when he realized I was alone. I couldn't relax or stop the tears as they poured down my face, washing away the lies, the perfect facade.

He stepped closer but hesitated, waiting to be welcomed.

"Yes." My voice cracked under the weight of my lie.

He sighed audibly as his hands ran over his messy hair and he stepped closer. "Nightmare?" He crouched in front of me, and I nodded, not wanting my weakness to show in my words again. "You want a glass of water?"

I shook my head because I felt like a fool. "I just need to catch my breath." I shoved the blanket all the way off my legs, loving the cool night air against the sticky sweat that clung to my body.

"You want to watch the sun rise?" His head cocked to the side, and I laughed because I was embarrassed.

"I'm sorry I woke you," I told him.

"You didn't wake me. I couldn't sleep either."

I wasn't sure if he was telling the truth or didn't want me to feel bad, but it helped, and I smiled.

"Let's go." Abel grabbed my hand and pulled me to my feet. I groaned, my head feeling heavy from the fog of the pills.

I glanced around the room. I'd slept on a single bed, and a dresser was pushed up against the opposite wall. It didn't seem like a permanent residence, but someone had to be spending a lot of time here. I was thankful they hadn't show up while I was sleeping.

"Let me grab my pants." Abel disappeared into the room where we'd smoked last night, and my heart sank. He had slept in an empty room on the hard wooden floor because I had fucked up…as usual.

"Were you supposed to sleep in the bed last night?" I asked, as I watched the muscles in his back pull and stretch as he bent down to pull his jeans on.

He grabbed a cigarette from his pack and lit it, turning to face me, his pants undone and riding low on his tanned hips.

"Nah. I was going to sleep on one of the couches, but our friends got a little crazy last night. I needed to be alone."

I nodded but didn't believe him, and I felt worse. He waited for me to leave the room and followed behind as we crept down the creaky steps to the front door. I glanced into the living room and saw a mass of blond hair and tangled limbs. I shook my head as I stepped into the fresh, warm air. The clouds were starting to fade into color as I sat on the steps and stared at the sky.

"I try never to be up early enough to see this." I laughed as Able sat next to me.

"I never seem to sleep through a full night." He looked at the ground, and I knew he had a story to tell, but it wasn't mine to hear. I barely knew him, and the last thing he probably wanted was a stranger prying into his business. I merely nodded, knowing exactly how he felt.

"How long have you known Trish?" I asked him.

He shrugged. "I don't really. I know *of* her. Adam has a big mouth."

"I say the same thing about Trish."

His lips twisted into a knowing smile, and he laughed quietly as he stared at the sky. I felt guilty for talking badly about her, even if what I'd said was true. Trish never would have argued about what kind of person she was. She knew; she just didn't care, and I envied her for that.

The clouds grew pink and purple, and the sky transformed into blue as we watched.

"Why Florida?" I asked, as I rubbed my bare legs, wishing again I had worn jeans.

"You tell me." He glanced at me, and neither of us was giving in, so I changed the subject, because that was how I dealt with things. I changed, adapted, and disappeared.

"Why don't you go to class?" I asked, and more silence followed as he pulled a deep drag from his cigarette and flicked it out into the grass.

"I learned all I need to know about life. I don't want to waste another second of my time."

"Wow. You're cynical." I laughed, but I got it and couldn't judge.

He leaned back on his palms, stretching out, his stomach soaking up the first rays of daylight. I tried not to look, but it was nearly impossible.

"I'm not giving up or anything," he said.

"I'm not judging…" My voice trailed off as I breathed in the fresh morning air tainted by Abel's smoke. There was nothing to really say. Our topic was too deep for strangers and the first light of dawn.

"Did you run from your problems?" I asked him. "Is that why you chose Florida?"

He sighed loudly, and I felt like I may have crossed the line, but I was honestly curious as to what could make one of the perfect people be so melancholy.

"I didn't run. I didn't choose." His eyes met mine, and I realized he wasn't comfortable with the direction our casual conversation had taken.

The sun was out from behind the wisps of clouds, and I already could tell today was going to be unbearably hot.

"You're stubborn." I sighed as my eyes fell closed, and I relished in the warmth of the sun on my face. My eyes snapped open with Abel's laughter.

"Like looking in a mirror, ain't it?"

I rolled my eyes, but I knew he was right. I was sarcastic and rude. Just add those to the list of my many flaws.

"Hungry?" he asked, and looked my way as I closed my eyes again, angling my head to the sky.

I nodded. I was starving but didn't want to bring it up. It wasn't my house, and I didn't think I could hold down cookies for breakfast.

"Let's go." He stood and held out his hand for me. I slid my fingers in his, hoping I wasn't pink cheeked from his touch. I let him pull me effortlessly to my feet, and I brushed off the bottom of my skirt. He gestured to an old black pickup beside the house, and I followed because I felt like if I went another hour without nourishment, I might wither away and die. I was a touch dramatic.

I slid into the passenger seat as Abel got in on the driver's side and pulled down the visor, causing a set of keys to drop into his lap. He shoved one of them into the ignition and twisted his wrist, and the truck to rumbled to life.

The radio was static, and he turned the knob a few times before an old rock ballad blared through the speakers. We rolled down our windows to let out some of the stuffy heat trapped in the cab, and I angled my head toward the open window, loving the wind blowing through my hair.

"This thing gonna make it?"

Abel laughed. "It's like the house."

"I get it." I held up my hand. "It's old and needs love or paint," I joked, and he sighed loudly as we picked up speed.

It was a brand-new day, and all I wanted was to forget any day before it. Abel didn't speak, and I was comfortable in his silence. He was a mystery, and I was curious but had to be careful not to reveal myself. Being one-dimensional was far less complicated.

We drove for only a few minutes before we hit a strip near the highway with a couple of gas stations and fast food joints. We pulled into a drive-through, and Abel turned down the radio so we could order. I wanted to fill the silence, but I was at a loss for things to say. Thankfully a voice rang out over the speaker next to his window, and he looked to me for my order. I asked for a breakfast sandwich and hash browns, and he ordered the same for himself.

"Wait! I should get something for Trish. She's going to be starving." I knew she hadn't eaten since before we'd arrived at the old house in the woods.

Abel smiled and turned back to the speaker. "Make that three."

The voice rattled off a total, and we pulled up to the first window.

"What about your friends?" I tried to keep my eyes from lingering on his bare chest as we waited for our turn to pay.

"They can take care of themselves. They're grown-ups."

I didn't know how to respond to that, but I realized I didn't have my purse, and now this stranger was going to have to buy my meal.

"I'll pay you as soon as we get back to the house, I swear."

His lip upturned into that delicious smirk, and his dimples settled deep into his cheeks. "You don't have to do that." We pulled up to the window, and he dug out his wallet from his back pocket.

"I can take care of myself," I said. "I'm a grown-up."

His grin widened, and he flashed me that heart-stopping smile as he shook his head, but he didn't respond. I watched as he grabbed a twenty from a thick stack of bills in his wallet, and the realization dawned on me.

"Oh, my God! You're their dealer! Why do you drive this bucket?"

The woman at the window gave me a sideways glance, and Abel clenched his jaw. He took his change and pulled toward the next window.

"I'm not a drug dealer, Delilah."

"Lie." I tuck my hair behind my ear.

"Are you doubting me or telling me your name?" His eyebrow raised again, and I realized he was being playful, the ghost of a smile on his lips.

"My name." I turned and looked out the window, hating that I always had to open my big mouth. I heard Abel getting the food and thanking the worker before we pulled off toward the house. He handed the bags to me, and I dug through to get our sandwiches.

"Thank you," I mumbled.

He took his sandwich and devoured it in three bites, and I couldn't help laugh. He didn't have an ounce of fat on his frame. He was muscles and tanned skin—all man.

Brock and I had started dating right after I turned seventeen. He was fit and strong but very much still a boy. There hadn't been anyone since him, and I was perfectly happy with that, but then Abel smiled and winked as he dug his hand in the bag on my lap to retrieve his hash browns. I felt my body heat up under the glow of the morning sun, and I hated myself for even thinking of another guy like I thought of Brock.

I took a few small bites of my sandwich, but guilt and memories stole my appetite.

"You should eat. Most important meal of the day." Abel turned up the radio, but it was only a low hum in the background.

"I had a huge dinner last night before we left," I lied, because it was what I did. It had become second nature since I'd become the new me.

"What did you have?" he asked, as he crumpled the paper from his hash browns and dropped it into the bag.

"Spaghetti," I said absent-mindedly, as I continued to stare into the nothingness along the road.

"Homemade?" he asked, and I turned to look at him with my eyes narrowed.

"Sure. With meatballs and everything."

He glanced at me out of the corner of his eye, and I saw his lips curve. He knew I was lying. How did he know that? No one ever questioned me.

"I hope there are leftovers." He was challenging me now. He wanted me to admit I was a liar. Who was this asshole?

"Of course." I reached over and turned up the volume on the radio. His hand covered mine, and our eyes locked.

"Good, because I think Trish mentioned something about us coming over today."

"Fine."

"Fine."

My eyes narrowed to thin slits, and I pulled my hand from under his. I huffed as I grabbed my half-eaten sandwich from the bag and unwrapped it, taking an angry bite. He turned up the song and sung along with a smile as we made our way back to the old house. Fuck this guy.

The house was still quiet when we returned. The door squcaked as we entered, and Trish turned her sleepy head. "We got you breakfast." I held out the bag and shook it, but Abel snatched it from my hand. I scowled at him as he dug out the hash browns from my meal that I didn't eat and took a huge bite then handed the bag back to me with a wink.

I rolled my eyes and pretended that my body didn't just kick into overdrive. My heart felt like it was exploding inside my chest.

"Thank you, guys," Trish mumbled, as she untangled her limbs from Adams. I tried my hardest not to make a sarcastic remark, but I felt embarrassed for her.

"God, did you at least use something?" I whispered, as she took the bag and shot me a dirty look.

"I'm not stupid. We just fooled around. What about you?" she mumbled, as she pulled her sandwich out and curled up on the smaller couch with her legs tucked under her body.

"I slept by myself as usual. You should try it sometime."

She rolled her eyes as she smiled. "Good, because I want my shot at Abel."

"Trish!" I turned around, but Abel was nowhere to be found, and Trish giggled.

"What?" she asked, and had the nerve to try to look innocent. I had no response. Abel was hot—anyone could see that—but it was her he had kissed last night during spin the bottle. The humiliating events flooded back into my hazy memory. I had made a total fool out of myself, and I could only hope that everyone had been too fucked up to remember.

"Just be safe." I had no argument. Trish's friendship was all I had, and I couldn't risk losing her. Besides, if I told her I liked Abel, I'd have to explain what had happened with Brock, and I wasn't ready to share that with anyone. It was better for everyone to assume he and I were still together. At least then I could explain away my tears when I was missing him.

"Keys." I held out my hand and waited for Trish to hand them over. I went out the front door to her car and grabbed my purse, digging out a ten-dollar bill to pay back Abel.

"Running away?" His deep voice called from the porch, and I jumped as he chuckled.

"No," I snapped, and slammed the car door shut. I marched back across the gravel toward him with my hand extended. "I was getting the money I owe you."

He shook his head as he blew out a cloud of smoke and didn't make any move to take the money. "You think if I had taken Trish with me this morning, she would have brought you food?"

My arm dropped to my side as I wondered what he was getting at. "She's too hungover to think clearly." I held out the money again as I tried to forget about her claim on Abel just a few minutes ago after I had made sure she was fed.

"Call it even. You're going to feed me spaghetti, remember?"

I sighed as I tried not to look frustrated. "There is no spaghetti. Are you happy now?" I rolled my eyes and folded my arms over my chest.

"So the truth comes out." His voice was laced with humor as he stared out at the yard.

"Yup. You caught me. I'm a big fat liar. Will you take the stupid money, so I won't owe you anything?"

Abel's eyes met mine, and for a moment, we stared at each other before he shook his head again and flicked his cigarette out in front of him. "No. You promised me spaghetti. You can't just break your promise."

"Are you enjoying fucking with me? Is it fun for you?"

"Is it fun for *you*?" His eyebrow rose flirtatiously. "I'm not fucking with you. Just trying to figure you out."

"Nothing to figure out. I'm not making you spaghetti. I'd tell you to ask Trish, but she wouldn't either, and no, she wouldn't have brought me breakfast." I dropped the money on the ground and walked around him to the front door. I had no reason to be so pissy, but I was really tired of playing the role of the sidekick, even if it was a million times better than being the outcast.

I tossed the keys to Trish, and they landed next to her on the couch. "Can we go? I need a shower." I heard the front door open and close behind me as Abel entered.

"You leaving?" he asked, and Trish sighed loudly and pushed herself up from the couch.

"Looks that way. Lie doesn't want to hang anymore." She shrugged, and I rolled my eyes.

"Mind if we swing by later?" he asked, and I spun around to look at him as Trish answered.

"Sure. Adam knows where we live."

I narrowed my eyes at Abel. "You're such a liar."

"That makes two of us." He winked, and I wanted to punch him in the eye so it would be permanently swollen shut.

Chapter Five

Lame Excuses

"Fuck! It's boiling all over!" Trish screamed, dragging me from my memories as spaghetti sauce popped and splattered over the stove.

I huffed and shoved her out of the way with my hip as I picked up the pot and held it over the sink as it cooled. "I was only gone for a second to change. What the hell happened?" I glanced at the stove and noticed the burner had been set to high.

Trish shrugged. "I thought it would cook faster if I turned up the heat."

I shook my head as I turned off the burner and dumped the sauce over the noodles. A knock came at the door, and I glanced over my shoulder at Trish, who went off to answer it. I heard the guys talking and Trish laughing loudly in that annoyingly flirtatious way she did whenever a man was near. I rolled my eyes and added the ground hamburger meat to my concoction. I wasn't the best cook, but I had learned early on that I would need to feed myself if I wanted to eat at all.

"Smells amazing," Abel said from behind me, and even though I didn't want to smile, I couldn't stop myself.

"Well, it sucks, so don't get your expectations up too high," I joked as everyone else filed in.

I nodded to Adam and Sean, who stood in the doorway.

Abel pulled open a few drawers until he found the silverware and grabbed enough for everyone. Trish got the dishes and set them out on our small table. There were only seats for four, but I was fine with not sitting with them. I wanted to lock myself in my bedroom anyway. I dished out a small portion for myself and set the pot in the middle of the table so everyone could help themselves. Adam, Sean, and Trish sat down and began rambling to each other about nothing in particular. Abel dished out his food and leaned against the counter next to me as he watched his friends talk.

"Sit," I said between bites, and he glanced at me before looking back at his friends.

"You sit."

I rolled my eyes but didn't move toward the chair, and neither did he. "You're stubborn." I took another bite.

"I could say the same about you." He wrapped half the noodles in his bowl around his fork and shoved the entire bite into his mouth.

"Are all people from California so rude?"

He shrugged. "Not as bad as the bitches from Mississippi."

"Burn." I rolled my eyes and turned around to put my bowl in the sink. I turned on the water and ran my bowl under it to rinse out the sauce. Abel turned around next to me, his side pressed against mine as he put his bowl under the stream, pushing mine out of the way. I pushed back, and a small laugh escaped me, even though I was trying my hardest to scowl at him. He glanced at me, a crooked grin on his lips.

"Fine. You can wash the dishes," I told him. I walked away, hating how frustratingly adorable he was. I lay down across my bed and grabbed my cell phone, finding "Wrecking Ball" on my playlist before putting on my headphones and closing my eyes.

I gave myself permission to imagine Brock's face—his eyes, dark gray like a storm cloud, charged and ready to wreak havoc; his hair brown like my natural color but buzzed short. His body was thick with muscles, and he was a few inches taller than me, so I would have to stand on my toes to kiss him. I smiled as I heard his voice calling me "Bird."

"This music is torture, Bird." Brock had a pained look on his face, and I couldn't hold in my giggle.

"It's not that bad." I hummed along to "When I'm Gone," which was playing on the radio in the gym at the shelter.

"You're killing me. We can't be friends anymore," he joked, as he bounced a basketball, the sound echoing in the cavernous room.

"If you stop being my friend, I will kill you." I took a step toward him. "Slowly…" Another step. "Painfully…" I snatched the basketball from the air and haphazardly dribbled it down the court as I laughed.

"You're cheating, Bird. You can't distract me with threats. I'm pretty sure it's frowned upon. Ms. Deb?" he called out to one of the workers, who looked over at us. "Bird is cheating."

I glared back at him and stuck out my tongue as I bent my knees and tossed the ball toward the basket. It bounced off the backboard and fell to the floor. Brock laughed so hard that he was clutching his stomach.

"Never mind, Ms. Deb. She sucks anyway."

Ms. Deb shook her head as she wrote on a clipboard she held in her hand. "Don't use that kind of language, Mr. Ryan."

"Sorry, Ms. Deb," he replied sarcastically, and I giggled as I chased after the ball.

The headphones were pulled from my ears, and I jumped, pushing up onto my elbows, as the storm in Brock's eyes was replaced with calm waters. "What are you doing in here?" I asked, as Abel took a step back.

"I didn't mean to scare you. I was looking for the bathroom. I thought you were sleeping, but you smiled, and I noticed the headphones." He ran his hand through his messy hair. "What are you listening to?"

"Your lame excuses." I rolled my eyes as I pulled my headphones off completely, and the dimples in his cheeks deepened.

He took another step back toward my door but stopped and turned back to me. "Thank you for dinner. It was great. I can't remember the last time I had a home-cooked meal."

I searched his face for sarcasm, but he was being sincere, and for a moment, I saw what looked like sadness in his eyes, but it was gone as quickly as it had come.

"You're welcome," I said, as he disappeared into the hallway. I put my headphones back on and replayed the song, but I didn't close my eyes. I could only take the memories of Brock in small doses without breaking down. I tried to focus on the good—his touch, the sound of his voice—but every part of my life back then was laced with the bad. I'd reached my limit for the day. I took off the headphones and tossed them onto my pillow, not sure what I would do with the rest of my night. It was Saturday, and that usually meant we'd be off at a bar or club somewhere. I hoped everyone would leave soon, and maybe I could relax with a good book.

I pushed myself up from the bed and made my way to the bathroom. As I opened the door, Abel turned toward the shower and zipped up his pants.

"Jesus! Shit! I'm so sorry." I yanked the door to close it, but he grabbed hold and pulled it wide open.

"Wow. Was it *that* disappointing?" He laughed, and my face burned with embarrassment.

"I didn't see anything." I was mortified.

"You really know how to hurt a man's ego."

"I didn't know you were in here." I couldn't look him in the eye, so I stared at the way his shirt stretched across his chest muscles, which only made me blush deeper.

"I just told you a minute ago." His eyebrow cocked, and I couldn't help scowl at him.

"Maybe I was ignoring you," I said. "It's hard not to block out your ramblings."

His head tilted to the side, and his fingers came under my chin to force me to look up at his face. "Lie."

"What?" I said, when he didn't continue after saying my name.

"*That* is a lie. You couldn't ignore me if you tried." He winked and walked around me before I could come up with a witty comeback. What an asshole.

I went into the bathroom and closed the door a little harder than necessary. I glanced into the mirror over the sink, and sure enough, my cheeks were tinted pink.

I splashed cold water on my face and forced myself to leave the safety of the bathroom. I headed to the living room to grab my Kindle, ignoring everyone.

"Lie, we're gonna go out for drinks," Trish called from the couch.

"Have fun." I began to walk out of the room as she giggled.

"No. *We* are going out for drinks. Get dressed."

I stopped walking and turned back to look at her. "I *am* dressed." I had on my favorite pair of torn-up jeans and a tank top. That was as dressed up as I felt like getting, but I knew by Trish's expression that she wasn't going to drop it. Heaven forbid I go out dressed like a normal person and embarrass her.

"Fine. Whatever. I'll change." I left before she could add any advice regarding what I should wear and went to my room. I stared at my closet, fighting back the urge to pull out my keepsake box. Instead I grabbed the first thing my fingers landed on, a thin gray dress that came up to my midthigh with a thick black belt around the waist. The color matched my contact lenses; I hated my plain-Jane brown eyes. I grabbed a pair of black strappy sandals and quickly discarded my old clothes and threw on my dress. I left my hair down and ran my hands through it to detangle it.

I stepped back out of my room only to find the three guys on the couch. Trish had gone to primp, and I knew we may have to wait an hour until she came back.

"Can I smoke in here?" Abel asked, and I shook my head. He pushed up from his seat and walked toward me. "Show me where?"

"Sure." I took him to the back of the kitchen, where our fire escape was. You could crawl out the oversize window to the landing. I spent a lot of time out there when I read or just to get some fresh air and sunshine. I wobbled on my heels as I climbed through the opening, and Abel grabbed my hips from behind to steady me.

"Sorry," he said, as he climbed out next to me, standing entirely too close to me on the tiny platform. I could tell from his playful expression he wasn't the least bit regretful.

He pulled a cigarette from his pack and held it out to me. I took it even though I usually only smoked if I was partying. He held a lighter to my face, and I inhaled as he lit it, his eyes locked on mine; he looked like he was deep in thought.

"What?" I asked, as I blew out a puff of smoke. He took the cigarette from me to take a drag instead of lighting his own.

"You don't really like Trish."

It wasn't a question, but I felt the need to defend my friendship. Yes, we were an odd pairing, but she helped me move past the person I was by allowing me into her life, and I wasn't a bully and wouldn't bad-mouth her to the boy she liked.

"I like her. We're friends." I shrugged and took the cigarette back. His eyes were trained on my lips as I inhaled. I hated his confidence and the arrogant way he spoke, but something under the sarcastic remarks kept me interested in who he really was.

"Friendship goes both ways," Abel said.

"Are those guys your *real* friends?"

He shook his head, his hand dragging through his messy hair. "They were there for me when I needed someone."

"And now? You don't need anyone? So...what? You just cast them aside?"

"I didn't say that." Just like that, the serious conversation had ended, and the flirty mask he wore was back in place.

"Why did you leave California?" I took another drag, but he grabbed the cigarette as it was at my lips.

"You ask a lot of questions. That's how I know you aren't like her. Do you think Trish gives a shit about where I came from?"

"Whatever. It's impossible to have a normal conversation with anyone here." I was exasperated. I moved toward the window, but he stepped to the side to block it.

I groaned but looked at him, waiting for a sarcastic retort. "You look nice," he said. I narrowed my eyes, but the punch line didn't come. Instead he leaned closer, his smoky mint breath on my cheek. "You looked just as sexy in those jeans."

My eyes met his, and I thought I was hallucinating, but his face was serious, and I immediately averted my eyes to the window. I pushed around him, and he moved out of my way as I slid it back open. As I climbed through, I couldn't resist throwing a jab at him. "Just not good enough to kiss, right?" I slid the window closed behind me before he could respond.

Trish was ready to go and waiting in the living room for us. A few minutes after I came in, Abel followed, and the popular-asshole persona was firmly in place.

"Let's go party," he called out, and his friends cheered and shoved each other toward the front door. I rolled my eyes but followed behind because that was what I did. I was always the extra wheel.

We made our way downstairs, and out front was a sleek, black Barracuda. Classic cars had a spot in my heart because that was all Brock ever talked about getting.

"We'll take my car," Abel said, as he pulled open his door.

"Much better than that rusty old truck," I said under my breath.

"There you go. Now you sound *just* like her," Abel replied just as quietly.

Trish made her way to the passenger side and slid into the seat. I waited for the other guys to climb into the back from the driver's side. As I prepared to follow, Abel slid the seat back and motioned for me to sit in the center of the front bench seat. "I can't let you sit back there with those fucking pervs. Your boyfriend would kill me."

I ignored his comment about Brock and slid across next to Trish. She looked less than pleased that she wouldn't be cuddling against Abel. I was the last person she should direct her frustration at. I didn't want to sit next to Abel any more than she didn't want me to, and it wasn't my fault she ran with such a shady group.

Trish leaned around me to look at him as we pulled into traffic. "You think you could hook us up before we get there?"

I glanced at Abel, who was working his jaw as he stared ahead at the road. "Glove box." He took a quick glance at me, and I looked at the glove box as Trish opened it and pulled out a bottle of pills. I looked back at Abel, who gripped the steering wheel so tightly that his knuckles turned white.

"Liar, liar," I said under my breath. I saw his head turn fraction of an inch toward me before he reached out to turn up the stereo and drown out any talk with classic rock music.

Trish pulled money from her wristlet and held it out to me. I grabbed it angrily and held it out to Abel. His fingers wrapped around mine and squeezed.

"It's on the house," he said, and his fingers slid from mine, leaving me holding the cash as Trish handed out pills to the guys in the backseat.

"Tonight is going to be epic, boys." She laughed as she popped a pill into her mouth and held one out for me. "Don't be such a baby."

I felt Abel's gaze burn my skin, and I held out my palm. He thought he was so smart. Everything he said was a lie, and he wanted to call me out? I popped the small pill into my mouth and swallowed. Trish let out a gleeful yell as Abel stepped on the gas and we flew down the highway.

Chapter Six

Party Hard

Domino was packed, and the strobe lights made the room feel as if it were tilted to the side. I giggled as I tried to navigate through the crowd on the dance floor. We barely could fit through the endless sea of bodies to get inside, but I didn't care. I felt weightless, free from the memories that plagued me. The lights flickered in a thousand different colors, and it was like slipping inside a rainbow.

Abel gripped my elbow uncomfortably as he helped guide me through the mass of people. Trish had her arms wrapped around his waist behind me, and I was desperate to disappear from them.

"I need to dance," Trish said from behind me, and I felt Abel's fingers release from my skin. I kept moving through the crowd, needing to blend in, like I'd done so many times before.

I had no idea what I'd taken, but it was making me feel like I was on a cloud. I wasn't a druggy, but in this world you have to be willing to adapt and overcome. I was adapting. For a moment I'd thought I'd seen something I could relate to in this stranger. Just as quickly it was all ripped away, and I knew he was no different from Trish, no different from the bullies who had spent years tormenting me.

I could be that way too; I could not care about anyone. So I set out on my mission to be one of the crowd. My skin tingled and ached as people rubbed against me as they danced. Soon I began to move with the steady, thumping pulse of the music, and my heartbeat took on the rhythm of the song. My body became languid, and I swayed slowly as the earth shifted with me under my feet.

Hands gripped my hips, ran over my arms, and trailed down my thighs, but I didn't stop. I couldn't stop. The affection I had craved was amplified in a tiny pill that made me feel like I was finally living, not just surviving. The fabric of my dress slid against my skin, and goose bumps followed. Hot breath tickled my neck, and beads of sweat were like tiny tongues flickering over my body. Time passed by on a plane of its own.

Seconds.

Minutes.

Hours.

Tick.

Tick.

Tick.

My skin grew hot under every fingertip, leaving trails of tingles and burns in their wake. I closed my eyes and moved with the flow of the body that was pressed against my back. I hadn't felt so much love pulsing through my veins since I'd been with Brock. Who knew love could be manufactured and bought and paid for?

The heat increased until I felt my strength slowly dissipate, and I was limp in my dance partner's arms, a puppet to his movements.

"You done?" a voice called sharply in my ear, and I glanced up to see Abel, anger in his eyes.

"Just getting started."

"I think it's time to go."

"Why? You got some more drugs to sell?"

He pulled me out of the stranger's arms. I stumble-stepped toward him, and my hands fell against his hard chest. My fingers slid over his button-down shirt, loving the feel of the silky fabric.

"Keep your voice down!" His tone was angry, and it made me pull back, but my balance was unsteady. Fortunately he kept his firm grip on my arm so I wouldn't fall over.

"Look who the liar is now," I teased with a half grin. I hated people like him, people like Trish, people like those in high school.

"I didn't lie." His cheek was against mine, and his breath blew over my ear. I closed my eyes, loving the silky softness of his flesh; the deep, soothing tone of his voice. "I thought you weren't like her."

My eyes snapped open at the anger in his tone, and I pulled back to look at him. "Like what? One of your customers? One of your friends? The liar is a hypocrite now."

"I'm taking you home."

I pulled back from him, but he refused to let go. "I don't want to leave, and I can't just leave Trish here. Some of us care about our friends."

"She isn't your friend," Abel said, and I fought the urge to cry because I knew it was the truth.

"Neither are you." I pulled back again, and this time he let me go.

"I'll make sure they get home." I narrowed my eyes as he rolled his. "I promise," he added, as the world pulsed and swayed like an ocean breeze around me. Abel's arms wrapped around my waist to hold me steady, and my head fell against his chest. The steady hammering of his heart beneath my ear soothed me, and exhaustion crept over my body.

"Whatever" was all I could manage, because I was lost in the feel of my body against his. He was taller than Brock, and his build was leaner, but if I closed my eyes, I could almost talk myself into believing it was him. He held me tightly as we made our way through the crowd toward the door. We stopped momentarily for Abel to tell his friends what he was doing. My body couldn't hold steady, and I continued to sway with the rhythm of the music.

Soon the cool night air surrounded us, and I opened my eyes as I was pulled toward the old muscle car in the parking lot. I heard faint whispers of "It's OK" and "I'll take care of you," and I clung to the safety and warmth. I slid over the slick vinyl seat of Abel's car then lay on my side. His hand fell on my shoulder, my head resting on the side of his thigh, as the car accelerated through traffic.

We drove for what felt like hours, and I faded in and out of consciousness until the car finally came to a halt.

"We're here." Abel's voice pulled me from my jumbled memories, and I pushed myself up to look outside.

"Why are we at the rape den?" I asked, as I took in the old crumbling house where we'd partied the night before. Trish's words made me laugh, and I covered my mouth to try to stop the outburst of laughter.

"Because I can make sure you're OK here," he said through clenched teeth.

Abel got out of the car, and I didn't move while he made his way to my side. The door opened, letting in a rush of night air, and I had to close my eyes to steady myself. He helped me from my seat and wrapped his arm around me as he guided me toward the dilapidated building. I wanted to protest, but his skin was alive against mine. The sensation was overwhelming, and I reached out to rub the hard ridges of his abdomen.

"You're stupid for taking that shit," he mumbled under his breath as he pulled my hand from his stomach.

"*You're* stupid for selling it."

His grip tightened, but he didn't argue as we walked up the creaky porch steps. He guided me up the stairs to the bedroom where I had slept the night before. My moral filter long gone, I unbuckled the belt from my waist as I kicked off my heels and pulled my dress over my head, leaving me in my beige panty-and-bra set. I collapsed on the bed, and Abel tugged the comforter from under my body and pulled it over me, his fingers brushing over my stomach as he did. I could barely make out his silhouette in the darkness. I grabbed his wrist to keep him from getting up, my body swimming in euphoria.

"I am *so* fucking stupid," was all he said, and his hot lips pressed against my forehead. My eyes closed.

That was the last thing I remembered before waking up several hours later in the darkness. A warm, strong arm held me captive against his body. I pulled against his grip as panic settled deep in my chest.

"I got you," Abel's deep, comforting voice whispered into my ear, but I struggled against him because he wasn't Brock, and my memory was a foggy haze. I had no idea what the hell we had done last night, and now I knew I could never be anything like Trish.

"Let go of me." I rolled over and was now face-to-face with him, my hands on his hard chest.

"I didn't do anything to you. I promise. You had a nightmare. I couldn't calm you. The only way I could get you to stop crying was to hold you."

"Where's Trish?"

"She's at home in bed…alone."

I sighed, my body growing slack against him. "Does she know where I am?"

After a moment of silence, he replied, "She didn't ask."

I allowed myself to be held by this stranger—the liar, the jerk. My body vibrated with silent sobs, and he held me as I broke down from the overwhelming feeling of loneliness. I cried out for Brock, cursing him for promising me forever and leaving me alone, but Abel's grip was relentless. I hated myself; I hated him, but he never eased his hold on me, and I needed his embrace more than anything.

I drifted in and out of consciousness and finally awoke for the day right before the sun rose.

"You can let go of me now." I squirmed against Abel, and his arms went slack as he yawned and I pushed up to sit. "Why are we even here?"

"You want the whole philosophical discussion about our purpose in life or the basics?"

"Shut up."

"You can hate me, Lie, but you can't do that shit anymore."

"What shit?" I asked, as I turned to face him, his face barely visible through the moonlight.

He propped his body up on his elbow and turned on his side. "Why would you *ever* want to be like her?"

"I *am* like her." I stood, wobbling under my weight.

"Liar, liar." My own words were whispered back to me, and I wanted to scream at him. Stupid stranger, asshole, nice guy. I pulled my dress on and slid my feet into my shoes. I searched for a few minutes until I found my belt and secured it around my waist.

I left the room and made my way on shaky legs down the steps to the front porch. It wasn't long before Abel joined me, a cigarette perched between his lips.

"You could offer me one." I didn't care if I was being bitchy. He laughed, obviously not caring as well. He lit his cigarette and handed it to me.

"You scared me."

I didn't know how to respond, so I didn't.

"Is this how you always are? You always take candy from strangers?" His tone was playful, but I knew he was asking if I was always this reckless.

I glanced at him then back at the moon. "No."

He nodded and stared up at the same vast night sky as I did. "I don't sell anymore. I wasn't lying."

"You think I'm that stupid?" I glanced at him, and his eyes met mine before looking back toward the moon.

"I don't think you're stupid, Lie. I think you judged me long before you got to know me."

"Facts, Abel. Facts. I took a pill that came from you last night."

I felt his eyes on my flesh. "I'm *so* sorry for that."

"Don't be. I liked it. It was nice feeling…" I was at a loss for words to describe how incredible I'd felt last night. "I felt full of love." I wasn't about to play a victim or let Abel know how much I regretted taking that drug. I wasn't a child. People didn't treat Trish like she had done something wrong, and they shouldn't treat me that way either. College was about making mistakes, trying new things without caring about tomorrow. I just wanted to be left alone while I fucked up my life.

"I used to sell," he said. "I had no other choice."

"There's always a choice," I replied quietly, my bitchy tone evaporated by his honesty.

"Yeah. I guess there is. Survive or lie down and die. I chose. Not something I'm proud of."

"Where'd you get all that money?"

His eyes met mine, and he seemed to be thinking over his response. The truth doesn't need to be thought over, so I just rolled my eyes and looked out ahead to the tree line. I was growing bored of the half truths and judgments.

"You really aren't going to let this go, are you?" he asked me.

I smiled because I knew he was going to cave. "Not a chance."

"All right. My parents had money. Lots of money. I never wanted for anything. But then I had to move in with my grandpa here in Florida when I was thirteen."

"Why did you have to move? Were you, like, a bad kid or something? Why wouldn't they make sure you had money to live?"

"It's your turn," he said.

"My turn to what?"

"What's your story? I know you're not like these assholes, so spill it. How did you end up with Trish?"

I shrugged as I stared at the warped boards of the porch. "I moved here to be with my uncle. We're practically strangers. My family never had money, but it's better here."

"Better how?"

"It's your turn."

He grinned and blew out a loud breath. "I wasn't a bad kid."

"That's it? That's all you're going to give me?"

"How long have you lived here?" he asked me. "If you didn't just come here for sunshine and college, then why?" He leaned back on his elbows with a groan.

"About a year and because I had no choice."

"We *always* have a choice, Lie," he replied playfully, using my own words against me.

"I made the wrong ones, I guess, and now here I am."

Abel flicked his cigarette into the yard as the sun began to peek out from behind the clouds.

"You're not making any better ones here." His eyebrow rose, and I lay back beside him on the porch as we stared up at the sky.

"That's the pot calling the kettle black." I smirked as I thought of having to explain that saying to Brock.

He laughed, and the boards below me vibrated. "Well, Kettle, I'm trying to make the right ones. It isn't always that easy."

"Nothing is ever easy, Pot." We both laughed then fell silent. "How did you get that scar?" I asked him, as I propped myself up on my side, resting my weight on my elbow, my head in my hand. My eyes scanned the pink-and-white line across his ribs that marred his tanned skin.

"Boating accident." His smile faded, and I waited for him to share more, but he didn't. He reached up and tucked my hair behind my ear. "I thought your eyes were gray."

"Fuck. My contacts. Did I take them out last night?"

He shrugged. "Brown suits you. It's like…the earth."

"You mean like dirt? Gee, thanks, Abel. I hate them. My mom used to say I was so full of shit that my eyes were brown."

"She sounds fun." He smiled.

"She wasn't." I rolled onto my back and squeezed my eyes shut to keep the tears from falling.

"Shit, Lie. I'm sorry." He was up on his side now, over me.

"Don't be. I should get home." I began to sit up, but Abel pushed my shoulder back down.

"Don't do that. I'm not as big of an asshole as you think."

"I don't think you're a *big* asshole." I grabbed his arm and pretended to examine his muscles. "I mean…come on. Do you even lift, bro?" My words dripped with sarcasm, and he shook his head and tried to hide his smile.

"Tell me what's going on with you and Brock."

"What?" I was caught completely off guard. "I don't want to talk about Brock, and it's none of your business."

"I held you for hours last night while you cried over him. The least you could do is tell me why."

"I just miss him. That's all."

He shook his head. "Did he…hurt you?"

"Are you serious? No! Of course he didn't hurt me. Brock would *never* hurt me."

"It's just…if I loved someone, I wouldn't be able to stay away from them." His eyes locked on mine, and his gaze fell to my lips, causing me to lick them. As our eyes met again, I pushed him back so I could sit up, and he didn't try to stop me this time.

"I really do need to get home."

"Let me grab my shirt." He stretched as he stood, towering over me. He had to be around six feet tall, and I felt small next to him.

He disappeared inside the house and came back a few minutes later wearing a deep-gray shirt.

"Good news! I found your contacts. Bad news is that they were on the floor."

"Ugh. I have another pair at home." We headed toward his Barracuda.

"Guess I didn't need to throw that pair on the floor then."

I reached to my side and smacked him on the stomach.

"It was a fucking joke!" He put his hands up to keep me from hitting him again as he laughed.

Abel pulled open the passenger door, and I slid inside and waited for him to make his way to the driver's side. I opened the glove box and pulled out the container of pills from last night, and my fingers bumped something hard. I lifted a stack of papers and pulled out a heavy silver gun. My gut twisted, and I froze with the weapon in my hand.

"Whoa. Let's put that back where we found it, sweetheart." He took the gun from my hand and slid it back in its hiding spot. I shook the bottle of pills, and his eyes narrowed and he took them too.

"Why do you have a gun? They're dangerous."

"Guns aren't dangerous. People are."

"Trust me…I know. *Why* do you have it?" I tried to shake the grim thoughts of my past from my mind.

Abel laughed and shook his head. "Been watching a lot of movies, Lie? You don't have to worry. I'm not going to hurt you."

"I'm not scared of you. I just want to know what it's for."

"It's for protection. It's to keep me safe, not to hurt anyone else."

"I'm starting to think you aren't a nice guy, Abel," I deadpanned, as I forced my face to go blank so he wouldn't see how much his having a gun bothered me.

"You think I'm nice?" His smile beamed.

"This is what I get for trusting strangers." I turned and looked out the passenger window as we pulled out toward the highway.

"Strangers with candy."

"You are *such* a drug dealer."

"You're nosy."

"Asshole," I mumbled under my breath to get the last word in. The guy who had held me all night and opened up to me about his past was gone, and the arrogant jerk from yesterday was back.

"You know, Kettle, if I didn't know any better, I'd think you're trying to hurt my feelings."

"Is it working?" I asked dryly as I looked at him. He was focused on the road ahead and didn't respond. I reached out and changed the radio station. He gave me a sideways glance but didn't change it back. In fact he sang along, and his voice was low and gravelly and downright sexy.

"Not bad. You ever think of quitting your drug-dealing day job and becoming a singer?"

"No, actually." His fingers drummed the steering wheel, but I thought it was more from nervousness than keeping beat with the song. "My mom was a singer. Not really my thing." He turned up the radio and switched the station to classic rock.

We pulled up outside my apartment building a few minutes later, and I yawned, dying for some caffeine.

"We could go get some coffee if you want," he said.

"I try not to consort with criminal types."

"Am I really that bad?" He stared at me for a long moment.

"Fine. Let me get Trish. I'm sure she could use the pick-me-up, and she's dying to spend time with you anyway."

"Is she?" he asked smugly. "I wouldn't have pegged *her* for the smart one."

I rolled my eyes and got out of the car, slamming the door behind me.

Chapter Seven

Smoke

The apartment was quiet, and Trish was draped over the couch, her arm over her eyes.

"How're you feeling?" I asked, as I made my way into my room and stripped off my dress and tugged on a pair of jeans and a tank top. I walked into the hall as Trish headed toward her room.

"Like shit. How do I look?"

"About the same."

"Whatever. You're such a whore."

I tried not to let her comment bother me. Trish had no idea that I was bullied throughout high school, and I knew she didn't mean it like they did, but it still made me want to replace her shampoo with hair remover.

"I can make you feel better," I called out, as she closed her bedroom door.

"How?" Her door popped back open, and she stuck her head out.

"Abel is downstairs, waiting to take us for coffee."

She beamed and closed her door again so she could get ready. I rolled my eyes and went into the bathroom to brush my teeth and fix my hair. I looked like hell warmed over twice. My eyes burned from being so dry, and I decided to leave out my contacts. It had nothing to do with Abel, I told myself.

Trish was ready in record time. She came out of her room in shorts cut high enough to show her butt and a tank top that she filled out much better than I ever could.

I followed her out of our place and down to Abel's car. She didn't hesitate to slide into the front seat, and I struggled to squeeze my way into the back. Abel's eyes met mine in the rear-view mirror, and he smirked, clearly amused by my discomfort.

"I'm dying for some coffee. You're my hero." Trish was primping her hair as we pulled onto the road.

"A hero? That's probably the nicest thing I've been called today." He glanced at me again, and I scoffed a little too loudly as I crossed my arms over my chest. I hated being the third wheel, but it was my perpetual place in this fucked-up world. I lived in the past and merely existed in the present, with no care for my future. That's just the way it was.

I sank back in my seat as I stared out of the side window, watching the world whirl by as Trish flirted with Abel and scooted herself damn near onto his lap. I slid over behind him so I wouldn't have to meet his eyes in the mirror.

"That was some good shit last night. You think you can hook us up with some more?" she asked, and I lay my head against the cool glass.

"No. Sorry. I don't sell anymore."

"Aw…come on." She pouted and pressed her chest against his arm.

"Do you smell that?" I asked, leaning forward so my face was between theirs.

"Smell what?" Trish asked, as she pulled her hair under her nose and sniffed it.

"Smells like smoke," I said. "I think something is burning. Oh, my God. I think your car is on fire!"

Abel pulled off the road and hurried out of the car. I pushed out from the backseat and stood next to him as he opened the hood and leaned over the engine to examine it.

He shrugged. "Everything looks fine."

"Are you sure? I still smell it." I shrugged, and he bent over further under the hood.

I leaned in next to him and whispered into his ear, "Maybe your pants are on fire, *liar!*" I grinned as he stood up quickly and banged his head on the underside of the hood. I couldn't contain the laughter that bubbled out of me as he rubbed the sore spot on the back of his skull.

"That's some commitment to a joke, Kettle. I'm impressed."

"The bump to the head was a bonus." I laughed. "That was karma."

"What do I have to do to make you believe me?"

"You could throw away the drugs, drug dealer."

"Fine."

"Really? You'd just throw them away? Why not give them to Trish then or use them yourself?"

"Because Trish would give one to you and—no offense, Lie—you're just dumb enough to take it again."

"Drug dealer with a heart. I'm touched," I replied dryly.

"I don't do drugs," he said. "Never have."

"So the pot and the painkillers?"

"Pot isn't a drug. Not when you get it for medical purposes, and those painkillers are for an injury I got during the boating accident."

"Oh…wait. Medical marijuana is legal in Florida?"

"No." He sighed. "But I did have a prescription in California. It's not my fault they haven't legalized here yet."

"I thought you've been here since you were thirteen."

"I went home for a funeral. It was a while ago, and I don't plan to ever go back. Are we done or do you need a blood sample from me as well?" he snapped, and I took a step back, wishing I knew when to shut my mouth.

"I'll settle for some caffeine and another bump on your head."

Abel tried to hold his scowl, but his smile won over.

"Should I get out or something? Is this thing on fire?" Trish called from her window, and I shook my head at her delayed concern for her own safety.

"We should go." Abel put the hood down and opened his door for me to slide into the backseat. I did and was thankful I'd chosen jeans today or my ass would have been right in his face.

After we pulled back out onto the road, Trish slid her body against Abel's and praised him for once again saving her day. He rubbed the back of his head, and I smiled to myself.

We pulled up to the coffee shop, and all I could smell was heaven. I didn't realize how exhausted I was until we arrived.

The Java Junkie was practically empty, with most college students still being in bed, so we were able to the score the coveted corner booth. Abel slid in, and Trish pushed in next to him, so I was left alone on the opposite side. A barista came to our table and took our orders, and we sat in awkward silence for a few minutes.

"So…" I said, and blew out a heavy breath.

"Last night was crazy, right? Where the hell did you end up? I always knew you had it in you." Trish winked. "That'll show Brock for never calling you."

I closed my eyes to block out her voice. It was too early, and I was dangerously undercaffeinated for this conversation.

"I didn't screw anyone." My eyes flicked to Abel and back to Trish, who was pulling sugar packets out of the dish on the table.

"Sure you didn't."

"I didn't," I replied angrily.

Abel cleared his throat and leaned forward, resting his arms on the table. He didn't mention where I'd been, so neither did I. I felt like he was challenging me to tell Trish the truth.

"I mean, I would have, but he couldn't get it up," I whispered. Trish giggled, and Abel's eyes narrowed.

"Can you really blame the *guy* if you don't turn him on?" His head tilted to the side.

"I guess not. I mean…he did seem kind of gay."

"Here you go." The barista dropped off our drinks, and I picked mine up and blew into the little drinking hole to cool it down a bit. She smiled at Trish, and I couldn't help laugh as she acted as if she were the only one around. Her beauty wasn't something that went unnoticed, unlike me.

"Turning men gay—is that like a superpower, or did it take years of practice?" Abel smirked as he picked up his cup and took a sip. The barista's eyes grew wide, but she quickly recovered, smiling brightly as she left the table.

"So…who did *you* go home with last night, Abel?" Trish asked casually.

"No one special." He stared across the table at me.

"Loser," I groaned, as I rolled my eyes.

"I may be a loser, but I *fuck* like a champ. You should try it sometime. Maybe you wouldn't be so cranky."

I wondered how Trish actually got home if he wasn't the one to take her, like he'd promised.

"Maybe we can go out again tonight…just you and me?" she asked him with a flirtatious grin.

I screeched as I tilted my cup just a little too far and burned my bottom lip.

"Sure. Sounds fun." I glanced up to find Abel's eyes on me and that shit-eating grin—the one he wore so often—firmly in place.

"Great. I know the perfect place." Trish rambled excitedly about her plans for tonight, and I was thankful when she had drunk enough coffee to stop talking and go to the bathroom.

"How did she get home last night?"

"Cab." He took a drink of his coffee.

"She could have ended up anywhere. You promised. You're a promise-breaking liar."

"Compound name-calling. Multitalented."

"Don't change the subject."

Abel leaned forward, his voice low and serious. "I couldn't leave you. You needed someone to look out for you, and Trish couldn't. I made sure she was safe. It's not like she hasn't done this a million times."

"So have I."

"No." He took another sip as he relaxed back in his seat.

"Yes, I have. All the time."

He shook his head. "When you showed up at the party the other night, you looked terrified, like you'd stepped into some hostel in a foreign country that drugs unsuspecting tourists so they can sell their organs on the black market."

"You got all that from one look?"

"It was one hell of a look, Kettle."

I relaxed back in my seat and drank a sip from my cup as Trish made her way back to the table.

"I just had the best idea." She clapped her hands together as she slid into her seat. "What if we hook you up with Adam? He's cute."

"I think I'd rather stay home and read."

"No one would rather read than have fun."

"Reading *is* fun," I said defensively, but Trish just giggled. "Didn't you already sleep with Adam?"

Trish's eyes went wide with embarrassment. Abel cleared his throat as his gaze danced between the two of us.

"I have some work to do, but I can pick you up around eight," Abel said, and Trish agreed with her pouty, overly pink lip pulled between her teeth.

"Where do you work?" I asked.

"Not a job, just work to do."

"Mysterious," Trish said with a smirk.

"More like suspicious," I mumbled into my cup.

Chapter Eight

Many Talents

The day dragged on painfully slow after Abel dropped us off at home. I took a long bubble bath and began a new book, but the hours crawled by. I don't know why I wished time away. It wasn't like tomorrow ever held something exciting and new. I wasn't working toward anything. I had college, but I had no clear direction and had decided to be undeclared for my freshman year.

I ate leftover spaghetti for lunch and saved some because I knew I'd be having it for dinner as well, since I'd be alone tonight. My phone buzzed beside me as I was sprawled across my bed, four chapters deep into my romance novel. I lifted it to find a text message from an unknown number.

How's the book?

I glanced around the room and back to my phone, thinking before typing a reply.

Who is this?

My phone vibrated again a few seconds later.

Am I that forgettable, Kettle?

I huffed and dropped my Kindle beside me on the bed.

Stalker.

The phone was quiet for a minute before another text rang through.

Those pajamas are hideous.

I flipped over and yelled as I saw Abel in the doorway of my room. I grabbed my pillow and threw it at him, but he just stood there, letting it bounce off his chest.

"Really? A pillow is your defense against a stalker?"

"What are you doing here?"

"I have a hot date tonight. If I'm lucky she might put out."

I rolled my eyes as I flipped back onto my stomach and grabbed my Kindle. "You don't need luck for that, but you may need a dose of penicillin."

Abel laughed and grabbed my pillow, walking it across the room and tossing it to the head of my bed.

"Where's Trish?" I asked, not bothering to look up from my Kindle.

"Changing her clothes."

"And how did you get my number?"

"Magic. It's one of my many talents—much like your ability to turn men gay."

"Is your first talent being a criminal?"

"That hurts. That really hurts, Kettle. You know, if you really want to be like Trish, you need to ditch the books and stop judging people."

"You're kidding, right?"

"I never joke about putting down a book," he said.

I was wrong. Abel's first talent was being sarcastic, and it was infuriating.

"So the perfect people have feelings too? I never would have guessed." I tossed my Kindle and pushed up from the bed. Abel towered over me in a charcoal button-down shirt and dark-wash jeans. His hair was messy as usual, and his appearance stopped me in my tracks. He looked hot as hell.

"Oh, no. Not feelings. Just a low tolerance for hypocrites, Kettle."

"I'm not a hypocrite, and stop calling me 'Kettle,' you asshat." I glared up at him, but his face was relaxed, and I swear I saw a smile tugging on his lips. He enjoyed getting under my skin.

He pulled up his sleeve and glanced at his watch. "This has been fun, but I have a date. Don't give yourself a paper cut, Kettle." He turned to leave, and I groaned with frustration.

"It's a Kindle, you idiot. There is no paper."

He pulled the door closed behind him, and I wanted to scream, but I just walked to my bed and sunk down on the edge. My door popped open again, and I looked up at Trish with Abel behind her.

"We're heading out. Don't party too hard." She laughed, and I glanced up at Abel, who winked before she pulled the door closed, and I was finally alone.

Once I heard the door to the apartment open and close, I walked to the kitchen and got a glass of wine. OK, it wasn't a glass; it was a coffee mug, and the wine came from a box. It didn't matter, because it did the trick either way.

I gulped it down and let the warmth spread throughout my body before I poured another and made my way to the living room. I plopped down on the couch and turned on the television. I hardly ever watched TV anymore, but the house was too quiet when Trish wasn't here.

I settled on the news and listened to the anchor ramble on about the government until my mug was empty and my eyelids grew heavy. I struggled to hold them open, but I soon gave in, and the anchor's face was replaced by Brock's.

"Are you going to sleep all damn day?" Brock whispered in my ear, and I startled awake, wiping my mouth to make sure I hadn't been drooling. I sat up and ran my fingers through my hair, trying to make myself look presentable.

"Shh. You're going to wake my roommate," I whispered, and pointed the mountain of blankets in the bed across the room. Heather had moved in late last night, and she didn't arrive silently. It took two of the workers to drag her in here, and they basically left me to calm her down. It took about an hour before her drugs began to wear off, and then she passed out, snoring like a chainsaw.

Brock glanced over his shoulder and smiled as his eyes met mine again. He brushed his knuckles lightly over my cheek, and I knew my skin blushed red under his touch. "You're beautiful when you wake up."

"Hardly." I pulled my covers off my legs and stepped out of bed. The tile was cold under my feet, and I looked around for my shoes.

"What is it?" he asked, as my eyes scanned the other side of the room. I held my finger to my lips and tiptoed to my new roommate's

side, searching around her bed. I crouched and ran my hand under the bedframe. When my fingers landed on my old sneakers, I grinned as I pulled them out and held them up for Brock to see.

"She seems like she's going to be fun," he joked, as I walked toward him and dropped my shoes on the floor. I grabbed his arm to steady myself as I slipped my feet into each one. "You want to get back at her? I could piss on her clothes."

I laughed a little too loudly. "You'd do that?"

"If it made you feel better, I would."

"Well, it doesn't. Boys are so gross." I let go of his arm and walked to the door, stopping to look back at Brock, who was eyeing the mass of blankets that hid my new roomie. "Come on."

He shook his head and followed me into the hallway. "You can't just let her get away with stealing your shoes, Bird. She'll think you're weak, and it'll only get worse."

"I know. I'll talk to her about it when she gets up."

"Yeah, talking will solve the problem."

"What do you suggest I do?" I stopped and turned to face him, frustrated that even in a place like this I was dealing with bullies. Brock reached up and tucked my hair behind my ear, his expression softening.

"Nothing. You're a good person, Lie. Don't ever change that."

I turned and continued toward the front room, where everyone was waiting to be taken downstairs for breakfast. Brock and I leaned against the back of the couch near the end of the line. Robert, a gangly redhead, leaned next to Brock, his freckled arms folded over his chest as he talked to another boy in front of him.

"He looked like he'd been hit by a fuckin' truck." Robert laughed as he replied to the other boy and nudged Brock with his elbow. Brock's jaw clenched, and he shook his head slightly but didn't respond. "Come on, man. Back me up here. It was hilarious."

Brock still didn't respond, and I leaned forward to look at Robert. "Who are you talking about?" I asked, and Brock stood up straight and turned toward him to block my view.

"Stop trying to start shit," he growled, which made Robert laugh nervously, but he didn't relent.

"My bad, man. I didn't mean to put your business out there in front of your new piece."

Brock's hand went around Robert's throat, and I saw the thin bones in the back of his hand protrude as he gripped tighter.

"Stop it!" I stepped between them and pulled on Brock's wrist. He reluctantly released his grip as he sneered, "What's wrong with you?" The line began to move, and Robert stepped around us to follow the others toward the steps.

"Nothing. Let's go eat, Bird." He grabbed my hand, but I pulled back, refusing to follow until I had some answers.

"Tell me who he was talking about," I pressed.

"You want to miss breakfast?" When I didn't respond, he groaned, lacing his fingers behind his head as he stretched his back. "He was talking about Keller, some dick who was in here before you showed up. We had a disagreement, and I fixed it. No big deal."

"You hurt him? Why would you do that? You're not like these guys, Brock. You don't need to stoop to their level."

"You're not like these fucks, but I am."

"You're a bully." I took a step back, wondering if all this time I was being played, part of some sick joke or a way for Brock to pass the time.

"Lie, I'm not like those assholes from your school. I would never hurt you."

"But you hurt other people. Why not me then, huh?"

He took a step closer as one of the workers yelled, "Last call for breakfast."

I raised an eyebrow at Brock, who made no movement to leave. "What makes you think I'd be OK with that?"

"Bird, the kid wasn't some innocent little fuck. He asked for what he got. I was protecting myself, just like I'll protect you." He took another step, and I didn't move away. "I never said I was perfect, but I'm trying to be a better person."

"I know you are." I avoided his eyes, but he ducked down to make me catch his gaze.

"You forgive me?" He put his hand over his heart, and I simpered, unable to be mad at the one person in the world who cared about me. His arms flew around me, and his lips brushed against my cheek. "I won't let you down, Bird. I promise."

I was startled awake by a hand on my shoulder, and my scream was muffled by Abel's hand over my mouth. His other held a finger to his lips to tell me to be quiet. I pushed up from the cushion and brushed my hair from my face as he knelt next to me.

"What the hell are you doing here?" I asked him. "What time is it?"

"It's early…or really late. I don't know. It's, like, three in the morning."

I groaned and flopped back down on the couch. "If your booty call is over, please lock the door behind you and make sure to visit your doctor within forty-eight hours."

"Wake up, party animal." He shook my shoulder, and I reluctantly opened my eyes.

"What could you possibly need that's so important at three a.m.?" I groaned, as I wiped the sleep from my eyes.

"*You* have a problem."

"I do, huh? This ought to be good." I sat up and stretched my arms over my head.

"Yes, you do. Her name is Trish, and she's fucking obliterated. We did a few shots, and she fucking lost it."

"Lost it how?" I was wide-awake with concern now.

"I was asking myself the same question until I discovered the pill bottle in my glove box was gone."

I rubbed my hands over my face out of frustration. "You've got to be kidding me."

"I never joke about—"

I waved him away to stop talking as I stood up from the couch. "It's too early for your bullshit. Can we tone it down until…let's say…five in the morning?"

He laughed and stood up next to me. "Fine. I'll take the couch. Be warned that I tend to sleepwalk when I'm drunk, so wear something sexy to bed." He stepped closer, and I put my hand on his chest to stop him.

"You aren't staying here."

"Kettle, I let you spend the night with me. It's only fair you do the same."

"What am I supposed to do about Trish?"

Abel lay out on the couch that I had just been curled up on and closed his eyes, not bothering to respond.

"Just great." I turned to go to my room.

"Good night, Delilah."

" 'Night, Abel."

I lay awake for the next hour, getting up to check on Trish every few minutes. I was terrified she was going to overdose or vomit all over the place. Her skin was pale, and she shivered like a puppy in the rain. I forced her to drink several glasses of water and eat a few slices of toast. She cursed and swatted at me, but I wasn't about to let her destroy herself. Eventually the weight of my eyelids won out, and I finally was able to get some shut-eye.

My dreams were a montage of childhood memories. I pictured my mother yelling at me to eat my cereal, and when I refused, she flicked the ashes of her cigarette into the bowl and told me I wasn't allowed to move until I learned to listen. She locked herself in her bedroom, and after what felt like a lifetime in my young mind, I did my best to eat around the gray milk.

My memory faded into Christmas morning at my grandparents' house. I couldn't have been older than ten as I sat perfectly quiet on the sofa. I heard my mom and grandma arguing in the kitchen over money. My mom was crying because she couldn't afford groceries, to which Grandma replied that she should have kept her legs closed. I didn't know what that meant at the time, but my mother's response cleared up any confusion. My stomach sank, and the red and green ornaments on the white plastic Christmas tree across the room blurred into a swirl of color. I heard my mother tell my grandma that if she wanted me, she could keep me. My grandpa snapped at them with a string of curse words before closing himself off in his den.

On the ride home from my grandparents', my mother counted out a stack of cash, and that was the last time we ever visited them.

"It's rude not to feed your guest."

I jumped. "Fuck. Abel, go the hell away." My eyes slowly came into focus on his bare, toned chest. They traveled lower, over the ridges of his abdomen to the delicious V that disappeared below his low-slung jeans.

"My eyes are up here, Kettle." His eyes locked on mine, and I knew I was busted. "It's five in the morning. It's officially time to start with my—what do you call it? My *bullshit.*"

"Why don't you go harass Trish?"

"I tried, but she yelled at me about needing her beauty sleep."

"She's *very* serious about her beauty habits."

"Duly noted." Abel grabbed my ankle and tugged me across the bed a few inches.

"I'm not the live-in help, Abel. Go make yourself some breakfast." I swung my arm blindly behind myself toward him but didn't connect.

"Careful there, Lie. You almost felt what a real man is like."

"You're a pig."

"The expression is 'hung like a horse.' You getting up, or do I have to carry you to the kitchen? Who let you women out of there anyway?"

"Ha-ha, very funny." I rolled over and gave him a dirty look before putting my arm over my face so I could go back to sleep.

"Fine. Have it your way."

I heard his footsteps retreat, and I sighed as I tried to drift back into unconsciousness.

"This is kind of hot, Lie." My eyes popped open and landed on Abel holding up a hot-pink thong. I'm sure my face was the same color as the tiny undergarment. I flew from the bed and snatched it out of his hand, slapping him on the arm.

"What are you doing, you pervert?" I whisper-yelled.

"Personally I liked that matching beige number you wore to bed with me the other night." His face was so close that we were breathing the same air, and he smelled even more like alcohol than when he'd come in earlier. His tone was carefree and flirty, but his grin was pure wickedness.

"Stop it. That's only for my boyfriend to see." I walked around him and opened my underwear drawer to shove them back in.

"Ah, yes. The boyfriend. What's his name? Broke?"

"Brock." I slammed my drawer and turned to face him, my back against the dresser.

"Right. Brock." He took a step closer, and I put my hand on his chest, his skin hot under my touch.

"How is it possible that you're even drunker now?"

Abel pulled a silver flask from his pocket and shook it. "You also had a fine sampling of boxed wines in your fridge. Very classy." His eyebrow rose.

"Only the best for guests who won't leave."

He looked down at his chest, where my hand was still against him, then back to me. I pulled my hand away and tucked my hair behind my ear. "You get even more obnoxious when you drink."

"Thank you."

"Wasn't a compliment." We looked at each other for a long minute. "Fine. I'll make you breakfast. Maybe it'll help you sober up."

He grinned in victory as I walked around him and toward the kitchen. I kept the light off and turned on the small one over the stove.

Abel took a seat at the table and stretched out his legs on the chair next to him. "Don't you want to know how I like my eggs?"

"No." I pulled open the fridge and grabbed the half-used carton of eggs and the milk. I placed them on the counter and grabbed some cheese and turkey lunch meat. If I was going to make breakfast, I was going to make it how I liked. I might add a little spit to his.

I grabbed a pan and set it on the stove then turned on the burner and cracked the eggs into a bowl.

"Don't you miss him?" Abel asked, and I sighed as I poured a little milk in with the eggs.

"Miss who, Abel?" I knew exactly who he was talking about, but I wanted to delay the inevitable heartache for an extra moment or two.

"I miss my family," he said.

His confession surprised me, and I turned around to look at him. "Why don't you go to California to see them?"

He laughed sadly. "My mom used to cook everything from scratch. It was crazy. Most people I knew had maids and cooks but not us. Mom wanted to make sure we ate healthy and weren't eating some bullshit fast food."

"Must have been nice." I turned back around and mixed the eggs with a fork.

"It was." I heard the smile in his voice. "Nothing like home cooking, right?"

"I wouldn't really know. I cooked for myself mostly, and it was never anything fancy. I lived off hot dogs and mac and cheese on the good days." I used the back of my hand to catch a wayward tear on my cheek as I grabbed the butter from the fridge.

"Yeah. After thirteen that was pretty much how it went for me too."

"Why did they send you here?" I glanced over my shoulder, and Abel was still smiling from the nostalgia.

"I'm not nearly drunk enough to go into that right now. Maybe some other time."

I nodded and went back to cooking our omelet. Abel's mood swings were giving me whiplash. One minute he was so frustrating that I wanted to scream, and the next he was coaxing tiny details out of me that I hadn't even told Marie. I felt like we had a secret in common, and that was enough to help me readjust the load on my shoulders and stand just a little taller.

"I hope you like omelets."

"I thought I didn't have a choice."

"You don't, but one way or another, you'll eat it. Makes it easier if you enjoy them."

"You're cold-blooded, Kettle. I love omelets."

I smiled to myself as I slid his omelet onto a plate and cut it in half. I nudged his legs, and he pulled his feet off my chair so I could sit down. I placed the plate between us and held out two forks. He took one as his dimples settled deeply into his sun-kissed cheeks.

"Thank you."

I nodded and took a bite as he did the same. The sounds that came from his throat were pure sin as he devoured his half. He began to steal bites from my side, and I threatened to stab him with my fork, but I let him anyway because I wasn't nearly as hungry as he was, and it was nice to have someone appreciate my food.

He didn't stop until the plate was clean. Then he relaxed back in the seat with his hand over his stomach. "That was amazing."

I grabbed our plate and forks to wash them, and Abel went into the living room. I heard the low hum of the television, and I guessed he had given up on sleeping at all. I turned off the light over the stove and made my way toward my bedroom.

"Lie," Abel whispered, and I turned to see him sitting on the couch, remote in hand and the soft light from the TV illuminating his face. He patted the cushion next to him, and I reluctantly went to join him. I knew it would be hell trying to get back to sleep, and I didn't want any more memories of my childhood flooding my dreams.

I plopped down with a cushion between us as he flipped through the channels. He would pause and glance at me for my reaction. If I didn't give one, he'd continue on.

"Oh! That's *Wild Things*. I haven't seen that in forever. Keep it on this." I pulled my legs up under me to get more comfortable.

We watched in silence, and it wasn't until about twenty minutes later that I realized how stupid my choice was. I kept my eyes focused on the screen as the infamous threesome scene played out. I felt Abel glance my way, and he readjusted the way he was sitting. It was embarrassingly awkward, but I relished in the fact that it was making him as uncomfortable as I was.

"So…" he whispered quietly. "You're kind of a perv."

I glared at him, and he laughed, but his smile faded, and what was on the television was momentarily forgotten. The sounds of moans and kisses filled the background, and my heart thudded loudly in my ears. I watched the lights bounce off Abel's face, the hard angle of his jaw more prominent and his blue-green eyes glowing from the dim lighting. My mouth became dry, and I ran my tongue over my lips as he swallowed, his breathing noticeably heavier.

"Kill me noooow," Trish wined, and our heads snapped in the direction of the hallway.

"I'll get you some aspirin." I jumped up from the couch, and I heard the channel switch to a talk show.

Chapter Nine

Wild Things

I cooked Trish an egg-white omelet as she snuggled on the couch with Abel. It wasn't an entirely selfless act because it afforded me a few moments of solitude while Abel was forced to listen to her incessant whining. She batted her eyes and stuck out her overly glossed lip, and he was putty in her hands, even after she'd stolen his pills. Men are idiots, and Abel was their king.

I cooked and hummed a song that had been stuck in my head for days, and after two verses, I realized it was the P!nk song Abel had sung in his car. Occasionally my personal concert was interrupted by laughter, and I angrily flipped Trish's omelet, causing it to split apart in the pan. Beggars can't be choosers.

I took Trish her food, and she didn't even thank me as I handed her the plate and took a seat on the mismatched blue recliner across the room. I turned my attention to the television, which was now back on *Wild Things*. I glanced at Abel, and he was looking at me, and even though the scene on now was innocent,

I felt the tightening in my belly that I'd had as we sat next to each other a few minutes ago. My eyes dared a glance at Trish, who now occupied my spot and was oblivious to my turmoil.

"What kind of cheese is this?" she asked.

"The kind you eat." I rolled my eyes as she continued to stare at me, and if she hadn't blinked, I'd swear she was one of those rubber sex dolls. "It's breast cheese."

"What?"

I kept a straight face as I turned toward her. "Oh, yeah. You've heard of headcheese, right?" I made a face like she was stupid if she hadn't heard of it, and she reluctantly nodded. "Well, this is breast cheese. It is all the rage in London. It's made from the breast milk of millionaire women."

"Seriously?" She dropped her fork as disgust washed over her expression.

Abel laughed but cleared his throat as Trish looked at him angrily. He nodded and pointed back to me. "I think I've heard about that. It's like…a delicacy, right?"

"Yes. That's it. It's a delicacy." I smiled brightly at Trish, who slowly picked up her fork.

"Yeah…yeah. I'm sure I've heard of it. Duh. I'm just… tired." She hesitantly took another bite, and I struggled to hold back a giggle.

Trish made a face as she chewed, and I looked back at the movie. "It's provolone." I sighed as I curled up on the chair and let my eyes go unfocused. I heard her mutter, "Bitch" under her breath, but I didn't care. I struggled to keep myself awake, knowing it would be better to go to bed early tonight, but my body disagreed. I faintly heard them in the background.

"We never got to finish our date last night," Trish said.

"Lie is right there." His voice had an edge of annoyance, but she didn't notice as she continued.

"She won't care. She's passed out." There was a giggle, and it sounded like they were readjusting themselves on the couch.

"Haven't you corrupted her enough?" Abel asked her.

"Come on. I know she's a wet blanket, but it's not like she's a virgin or something. She has a boyfriend."

I tried to hear the song that had been stuck in my head, but I couldn't get it to drown out the sound of their voices.

"Has anyone actually seen this mystery boyfriend?" Abel's voice was soft, but it cut through me like a hot knife.

Fucking jerk. I resisted the urge to jump up and run to my room. It would just be more humiliating. I felt the sting of warm tears, and I turned my head ever so slightly into the back of the chair. At least I was facing away from them; it was my only reprieve from this degradation.

"He's probably not even real." Trish giggled, and I hoped she choked on her omelet. There was more rustling around.

"She's gonna wake up," Abel said.

"Fine. Come to my room." There was a pause then the sound of footsteps down the hall and the quiet click of Trish's bedroom door closing, or maybe that was my heart cracking. I couldn't be sure.

As soon as the coast was clear, I tiptoed to my room and closed the door. I made a beeline for the closet and dug out my box of secret memories. It held all the happy moments of my life, and it was no bigger than a shoebox.

I slid off the lid and made my way to my bed. I crossed my legs as I sat in the center and pulled each item out as I recalled the exact moment in time it had come from.

First was the picture of Brock from the shelter that he had stolen from his file. I stared at his black-and-white image as I recalled helping him choose which shirt to wear that day, only for it to be ruined by Tommy Larsen's blood when he got hit in the nose with a basketball during our exercise time.

I pulled out another item. It was a small scrap of paper that simply read, "Bird." I held it against my chest as a smile pulled at my lips and tears stung my eyes.

I took everything out and surrounded myself with Brock's love. I put in my earbuds and played sad songs to drift off to sleep so I wouldn't have to hear what was going on in the next room.

"I want to kiss you, Bird," Brock whispered in the darkness of my room as he held me in his arms.

"No." I giggled and pulled back from him, but he held me tightly against his chest as he glanced at the closed door, which we stood only a few feet away from.

"Why not?"

"We'll get in trouble if someone finds us in here in the dark." I pushed lightly against his chest, and he reluctantly released me, taking a few steps back to turn on the light and pull the door open. He'd still get in trouble for being with me, but it wouldn't look nearly as bad. I took a few steps back and sat on the edge of my bed. I gestured to my roommate's bed with my chin.

Brock's gaze followed mine, and he shoved his hands into his pockets. "What?" he asked, and I narrowed my eyes.

"Heather flipped out this morning because someone stole all her underwear."

"Probably the first time anyone touched her skanky panties."

"Oh, you're hilarious. Guess who had to deal with her meltdown?"

Brock didn't say anything; he just ran his hand over his hair as he bit back a laugh.

"Oh, you think it's funny?" I grabbed my pillow and tossed it at him. He caught it before it hit his chest and tossed it gently back to my bed. "You said you wouldn't do anything."

"Bird, where I come from, if someone steals your shoes, they catch a beatdown. She got off easy, and I bet she won't do it again." He raised an eyebrow as he casually strolled toward me.

"You can't fight my battles for me."

His hand ran through my hair before his fingers tangled into a fist, and he gently pulled my head back so I'd look up at him. "You can't just sit back and let people walk over you. You don't deserve that, and I'm not going to sit back and watch as it happens. You mean too much to me."

"Oh, yeah?" I asked playfully, as he bent down and pressed his lips against my forehead. He breathed in deeply before pulling back.

"You have no idea, Bird." His forehead rested against mine, and I let my eyes fall closed. "No idea."

The music stopped, and I blinked myself awake. Abel held my phone in his hand, and he placed it next to me and picked up a picture of Brock.

"Mystery solved."

I sat up and snatched the picture from his hand. "Go home."

"I was just leaving. I wanted to say bye. I'll see you Tuesday."

"I won't be here."

"Where will you be?"

"Not here," I snapped, as I rolled away from him.

"All right. I'll see you around then, I guess."

I didn't say anything, and his eyes danced over the mementos one last time before he left. It took only a moment for his annoying presence to be replaced with Trish's.

"Oh, my God!" she squealed, and I stared down at the picture of Brock so she couldn't see how much what she'd said in the living room had hurt me. It didn't matter anyway. She wouldn't care. "Abel's fucking hot, right? I mean, like, epic fucking hotness."

"Yeah, if you can get past his horrible personality." I glanced up at her, and her hands were on her hips. "Right. He's perfect for you."

"I know! I mean, come on. He's like sex on a freaking stick."

"I'm happy for you. You guys deserve each other."

"Thanks, Lie." She squealed again and left my room so I could sulk in private. I grabbed my phone and sent a quick text to Marie.

I put everything back in my box and hid it in the closet before Marie responded and told me she'd be at her office in half an hour.

I forced myself to shower and make myself presentable. I wasn't the biggest fan of makeup, but it was all part of the new and improved Delilah.

The walk to Marie's office was quick, and there was hardly anyone around since church hadn't let out yet. The door to her office was locked, so I knocked and waited for an answer. She pulled it open with one hand as the other secured a barrette in her hair.

"Sorry it took me so long," she said. "I slept in this morning, and traffic was hectic."

"No worries. Sorry to bug you on your day off." I stepped inside and waited for her to lead me to her private room.

"It's no problem, Lie. I'm glad you want to talk."

Marie took her usual seat, and I walked over to the window, not wanting to look her in the eye as I spoke.

"What happened?"

"I don't like it here."

"I thought you liked Florida better than Mississippi."

"Things change." I glanced over my shoulder at her, and her eyes were on me, a notepad in her lap and a pen between her fingertips.

"What changed?"

"I obviously didn't. I'm still me on the inside no matter what I do."

"You can't judge your self-worth by the opinions of others."

"Sometimes I wonder if it all ever happened, ya know? Maybe I made it all up. Maybe I'm the crazy one."

"Most people with mental illness don't know they have it, so the odds are in your favor."

I looked back again, and Marie was smiling. "Are you allowed to make jokes?" I asked her. "Isn't that against the therapist superhero code?"

"I won't tell if you don't."

"Secrets are what I'm good at." I looked out the window to the palm tree just outside. The bright-green fronds hid the dead brown ones below. It was kind of like me. The makeup and stylish clothes hid the ugliness underneath. "Brock thought it brought us closer, keeping secrets from the world."

"What did you think?"

"We didn't have much of a choice." I shrugged as I dragged the pad of my index finger down the glass. "I think it was a positive way to look at things."

"Was Brock a positive person?"

"That depends on who you ask."

"I'm asking you."

I made my way to my seat, noting the chessboard was gone, replaced with checkers. I snorted. "I take it none of your patients knew how to play?"

"Tell me a positive memory about him," Marie prodded.

"He was my first kiss." I smiled as I drifted back to that day in the shelter.

"Why are you sitting over here all by yourself?" Brock asked, as I stared at the floor of the main lounge, not wanting him to see my face. I knew my skin was blotchy and my eyes swollen from crying. He crouched in front of me with his arms resting on his knees for balance. "Have you been cryin'?"

I glanced up to look at his face as I wiped my palms over my cheeks. His eyebrows pulled together, and his stormy gray eyes reflected my own sadness.

"Stop that," I whispered. "Stop looking at me like you pity me." My gut twisted in embarrassment, and I wished I could run away from here. I let my long hair fall in front of my face so I could hide behind it.

"I'm not. I swear. I just want to make it better. Are you missing home again?"

I shrugged as my eyes danced over his hair because I didn't want to look him in the eye when he answered with some rude remark.

"If your mom is so damn mean to you, why aren't you happy to be away from her?" he continued. "You're here with me."

"I'm not crying over my mom, and trading one cage for another isn't exactly a step up."

"Then why are you crying? You've got give me something. It's not like you can run away." His muscles tightened in his face as he clenched his jaw. I remained silent as I looked him over. He was cute, and it pissed me off, because I knew outside of this hellhole he

wouldn't give me a second glance, and soon we'd both be out in the real world.

"Fine. Have it your way." He moved next to me and took a seat on the floor, groaning as he relaxed his head against the wall.

"Just go away." I whispered, and he turned his head to face me.

"So you still can talk. I was worried you'd stroked out on me for a second, Bird."

I smiled despite trying to keep my scowl in place.

"She smiles too." His hand went over his chest. "Now I'm the one who's speechless."

"Oh, wow. That was lame." I rolled my eyes, but my smile grew, and I glanced at him as I tucked my hair behind my ear.

"You're harsh. I didn't know you had it in you, Bird."

"Thank you."

"For what?"

"For talking to me," I told him. "I know you didn't need to waste your time in here with me."

"Is that what you think? I've wasted my time?" He stretched out his legs, but his face didn't relax.

"You know you have. I'm going to be out of here soon, and it would be social suicide for you to show your face with me in school."

He laughed loudly, and I couldn't help join in. People turned to look at us as we disrupted whatever mundane activity they were doing. "You think I give a fuck what anyone thinks about me?"

"You honestly don't care if people make fun of you for being around me?"

He smiled as he shook his head. "All I care about is what you think. What do you think, Bird?"

"I think you'll change your mind once we're out of here." My eyes drifted over his black shirt, which was stretched tautly across his thick chest.

I ran my fingers through my dark hair, my fingers getting snagged in a snarl, and I groaned in frustration.

"It's that quail soap or whatever the hell they call it. All the girls walk around here with messy-ass hair. Don't worry about it."

"Mine kind of always looks like this." I raised an eyebrow.

"It suits you. Makes you look wicked crazy," he joked, and I smiled, despite my sadness.

"I'm not crazy."

"You sure? Well, I'll make you a promise. I won't tell anyone you aren't bonkers if you don't tell them I'm really a nice guy."

"People are only nice if they want something." I pushed myself to my feet and stretched. Brock stood up beside me, and I walked back around the corner and down the long hallway that housed the bathrooms and bedrooms.

"This again? What do you think I want from you?" His gaze flicked to mine, and my cheeks burned under his stare.

"I don't know," I said. "We barely know each other."

"What do you want to know?" he asked, as he watched one of the girls walk by us and down the hall to the main lounge.

"Why did you run away?"

He sighed and ran his hand over his face as he slowed his pace. "This really isn't going to help my case in making me look like a good guy, Bird." He chuckled. "Well, I ran with a pretty crazy group of guys in Boston. They liked to take shit, cause fights. It was a tough neighborhood. You had to either fit in with them or be one of the pussies who got their asses beat to fund the next ripper."

I drew my eyebrows together as he shoved his hands into the pockets of his jeans. "A ripper is a mad-cool party."

"Wow, sounds like a great place. I can see why you wanted to go back."

"It's all I know, and after Laurie…this place is too…quiet."

"It's not that quiet for all of us." I rolled my eyes and turned to walk back toward the main room.

"Someone fucking with you?" He put his hand on my shoulder to stop me from walking. "Lie, if you tell me, I can take care of it for you."

I started to walk again, and he followed beside me. "I don't need you to fight my battles for me, and I highly doubt you want to take this one on anyway."

"What? You think I can't protect you?" Brock laughed and shook his head. "No faith in me at all, huh?"

"You see that overgrown jerk standing in front of the couch?" I motioned with my chin as we reached the end of the hall. "He told me this morning that I need to pay their dues."

"What the fuck does that mean?"

I shrugged as I let out a loud breath. "Judging by the way he was grabbing himself, it wasn't hard to guess."

Brock was halfway across the room before I could call out his name. He was piss and vinegar, pure testosterone and no outlet. He didn't care what anyone thought, and I envied him for that. More than anything, I wanted not to give a shit about anyone else's opinion, and I wanted to be tough like him.

"This fucking guy? This is the guy who thinks he can threaten you?" he yelled, his voice deeper than it had been a minute ago. "You trying to call hosies on Bird?" he asked the guy, looking up to him because he stood at least half a foot taller than him. Brock's Boston accent came through thickly with his anger.

"I was just fuckin' with her." The kid waved his hand as if to dismiss Brock, which only infuriated him more.

"Now I'm fuckin' with you," Brock told him.

One hit was all it took, and the heavyset kid fell over the back of the couch and slid to the floor as blood oozed from his nose. Everyone screamed, and it was deafening in the small space. Brock turned back to me with a grin as the staff grabbed hold of him and struggled to keep him contained. "You have faith in me now, Bird?" he yelled over the commotion.

I stared at him, slack-jawed in shock, as he beamed with pride. "Bird?" he called out louder, and jerked his body, causing the shelter staff to lose their hold on his right arm, and he pulled toward me.

"Yes," I called out over the chaos, and he relaxed for a moment as he stared at me.

"Mr. Ryan, you need to calm down," one of the women yelled into to his face, but he didn't acknowledge her.

"Bird, I'm going to kiss you right now. Do you believe me?" He wore a playful smirk, the anger in his voice gone. He had tried to get me to kiss him for weeks, but I'd turned him down, afraid he'd be able to see that I'd never done it before.

I couldn't help laugh at the insanely silly mood he transformed into. He was crazy; in fact he had to be certifiably crazy. I nodded once, my hands clasped in front of my chest. It was like a magnetic pull. He twisted free and pried another hand off his shoulder before he took off, nearly tripping as he weaved through the crowd. The other kids darted out of his way just in time to not get bowled over by the staff. Brock stopped in front of me and grabbed either side of my face in his hands and pressed his lips hard against mine. The world stopped and sped up at the same time, just like my heart. His tongue slid over the seam of my lips, and I let them part, welcoming him to deepen the kiss. My tongue followed his lead, pushing gently against his as my arms slid around his waist.

Two staff members pulled him back, but he kept his hands on me for as long as possible until his fingertips slid over my cheeks and grasped at the air.

"When I say something, I fucking mean it," Brock called out with pride as they took him around the corner to the stairs, and like that he was gone.

I looked up at Marie. "I know it seems crazy, but everything was at that time. We were locked away from the world, stuck in limbo. Everyone was scared or angry, and most just gave up on giving a shit. Brock gave me something to look forward to when I woke up. I didn't cry again while I was in there."

"What was the significance of his nickname for you?"

I smiled so hard that my cheeks hurt. I'd never had a boy show interest in me, let alone risk everything just to show me he did.

"Bird." I let the word roll off my tongue as I tried to remember how it sounded coming from his lips with that thick accent. "I asked him a million times to tell me, and he always refused until after that fight. I think he liked it when I bugged him about it. He thought it was cute when I was frustrated." I let out a laugh. "Boys can be really stupid."

It had been two long days since I'd seen Brock, but my lips still tingled from his kiss, and my heart fluttered every time I thought of him. No one in the shelter came near me, and I couldn't have been happier. I'd rather be left alone than deal with any more bullying. I got enough of that from school, but the days dragged by like years.

We all sat down to lunch, just like every other day, and while people groaned and bitched about what they served, I was in heaven. It was nice to know a meal was coming. Everyone chatted as they ate, except me, who daydreamed about my first kiss as I bit into my meat loaf. The sound rumbled to a low whisper and stopped, and that's when I saw him. Brock was back, no longer in the shelter's version of solitary confinement, which consisted of his being kept in his room. He searched me out, and when his eyes met mine, he grinned wildly as he made his way to my side.

"Did you miss me?" he asked playfully as he sat next to me on the bench.

"Yes. You're the only one who talks to me."

"You can't let them bother you, Bird." He tucked my long dark hair behind my ear, and I rolled my eyes at him. It wasn't that simple; nothing is that easy. If I could shut off my feelings, I would have done it years ago. "All we need is each other. Fuck these guys. They don't get a say in our happiness."

"Why do you keep calling me that?" I'd been in a foul mood ever since they'd taken him away.

"I can't give away all my secrets, Lie."

"Whatever."

"Don't be like that. I'm just messing with you. You're my little jailbird." His grin made my heart go insane.

"It isn't jail, Brock." I rolled my eyes as he laced my fingers in his under the table.

"Your home is your jail, Bird. I'm going to set you free." He picked up the apple from my tray and took a bite.

"Really?" I turned to face him.

"Do you need me to prove to you again that I mean what I say?"

"I think you proved that point, although I'm not so sure you're really a nice guy," I quipped.

"I think you'll like Boston."

"You want to take me to Boston with you?"

"You think I'd leave without you?"

"How will we get there? It's really far."

Brock dropped the apple onto my tray and rubbed his hands together. "I'll figure it out. It's gonna take a lot of cash."

"I can't help with money. My mom is broke."

His shoulder bumped against mine. "Like I said, I'll figure it out. Don't worry. But it'll probably take some time."

"It didn't bother you that he used violence to show you he liked you?" Marie asked me.

"People used violence to show me they hated me. What's the difference?"

"Are you sure you weren't looking past something that you knew was wrong because it felt good to get attention from a boy?"

"He wasn't just any boy. He was *the* boy."

"Explain."

"No one bullied Brock," I said, "and no one came near me once they knew he was watching over me. It was just like those fairy tales you hear as a kid."

"Fairy tales don't usually include getting locked up in a youth shelter and witnessing random acts of violence."

I shook my head. "You don't get it. You've never been me."

"Everyone is fighting a battle, Delilah. "

I pushed up from my seat in anger, a side effect of having spent so much time with Brock. "That's bullshit, and you know it. Brock is the only person who ever cared about me. So he got in a fight. Big deal. Kids get in fights all the time. At least he wasn't being the bully. He was standing up for me."

"Please calm down, and let's take a short breather. Then we can try to work through this so I can see your side of things. Sound good?"

"Yeah." I nodded and made my way to the front door of the building. I grabbed a cigarette from my pack and lit it, pulling a long drag of smoke into my lungs. My eyes closed as I exhaled.

I knew Marie was right, and it pissed me off. Brock had saved me. I was hanging on by a thread, and he had held on to me and made sure I didn't fall.

I glanced over my shoulder before descending the stairs and heading down the street to my apartment.

Chapter Ten

Asshole

I was angry at everyone, and I was sick and tired of being a doormat. Nothing had changed since high school, not since Brock had been taken away from me. Bullies don't grow out of it; they just get older, and I grew more tired.

I walked into the house, ready to tell Trish that she was a slut and that I'd heard what she had said about me, but I found her passed out cold on her bed with a baggie of something white by her head. I almost shook her awake, but instead I grabbed the car keys on her dresser and decided to direct my anger at someone else.

Maybe it was because Abel had pretended to be nice to me. Maybe it was because he had me fooled that he was like Brock. I don't know what I saw in him that reminded me of my past, but I couldn't let it go. I sped down the highway, weaving in and out of traffic as I pulled my phone from my pocket and sent a quick text to Abel.

Where would I find an arrogant prick at noon on a Sunday?

I dropped my phone and continued toward the old house, and after a minute or two, he replied.

How would I know how Donald Trump spends his weekends? Shaving orphans for a new toupee is my best guess, Kettle.

I groaned and sped up as I made my way down the back road to the decrepit house. The black muscle car was nowhere in sight; the old pickup truck was parked in its place. I got out, slamming the door, and Abel stepped onto the front porch, his T-shirt gone and an old shop rag in his hands as he wiped them together. He came down the front steps, his brow furrowed as I stormed toward him with fire in my veins.

"You're an asshole," I yelled, as we closed in on each other.

"So it *was* me you were talking about in the text."

As I reached him, I poked my finger hard into his tanned chest. "You think you're so fucking funny, don't you?"

"Do *you* think I'm funny?" His brow lifted, and I wanted to scream.

"I think you're a fucking jerk."

"Kettle, calm the hell down and tell me what's wrong."

"What's wrong? Really? In a matter of days, you've *ruined* everything. I was fine with being the sidekick. I was accepted. I finally fucking belonged in the stupid bubble you and all your jackass friends live in."

"Whoa, don't lump me in with those assholes."

"Don't be cute."

"You think I'm cute?" The side of his mouth pulled up in a smile, and I fought back the urge to slap him.

"Shut up," I yelled, exasperated. "Why did you have to humiliate me in front of Trish during spin the bottle? You made me look a like a fool. Then you keep putting the seed in my head that she isn't really my friend and that she's using me, and the icing on the fucked-up fucking cake is you and her making fun of me then me having to listen to you fuck her right next to my goddamn room!"

I was out of breath, and my chest rose and fell rapidly as I struggled to get a grip on myself. I knew I should be mad at Brock. I knew this was all my own doing, but I wasn't ready to accept responsibility for any of it.

"Can I talk now?" Abel paused, and I nodded like a bobble-head because I had no fight left in me. I could hear how stupid I was acting as the words left my mouth, and now I couldn't take them back. "I didn't humiliate you in front of a girl who'd just been passed around between three fucking guys. I knew you were better than her, and I wasn't going to let you compromise your integrity for a bunch of *assholes* like us. There's also the matter of your boyfriend. I didn't want you to hate yourself for doing something you'd regret, and—let's face it, Kettle—I'm the type of guy you'd regret."

Abel stepped closer, and his chest pushed against mine as his breathing grew as ragged mine. "Second, Trish isn't your real friend, and you fucking know it. And no matter how much you try to pretend you're like her, I see through it. You *do* care about her, and you're wasting your fucking time. You may not see it, but you're better than her."

He was right. She wasn't my friend. Oh, God, he was right. I felt like I was going to be sick. I could only hope this humiliation would end soon. Abel's voice lowered, and I could tell he was trying to compose himself. "I wasn't talking shit about you.

That was Trish. I just wanted to know what Brock did to you. It wasn't my place, and I should have known you wouldn't have confided in her, but I was fucking curious because I've seen you cry over him. It's not right."

"If I wanted to tell you, I would have." My voice was small, defeated.

"Third, I didn't fuck Trish. I'm not into girls throwing themselves at me. It's not very fucking attractive."

"Then why did you go into her room?" I tried to stand taller, to match his height, but I still had to bend my head back to look up at him.

"I didn't want you to wake up to your *friend* trying to fuck me on the couch five feet away from you."

"Why do you even care?"

"Because she wasn't the one I wanted to kiss during that game. No one here has ever tried to get to know me. All they ever want is to find their next high. I thought you were different, but it didn't matter because you're hung up on some asshole a thousand miles away." He took a step back, and now he was the one who looked pissed. "Go home, Delilah." He turned back toward the old house.

"What happened to 'Kettle'?" I called after him.

"You tell me," he yelled back without turning back around. He disappeared inside the house, and my shoulders sagged in defeat.

"Way to fucking go, Lie," I mumbled, as I got back into Trish's car and left.

I arrived home to a still-sleeping and none-the-wiser Trish. I was thankful that I at least had another day to wallow in pity before it all came crashing down and I'd be on a bus to nowhere. By nighttime I had myself convinced that Abel was going to be long gone, and Tuesday would be like every other worthless day in my life. He had to be growing tired of his relationship with Trish. Guys like him didn't get attached. It couldn't be too long before he was nothing but a memory.

I fell asleep to images of a very different version of spin the bottle and awoke to the still-dark sky. I slipped out onto the fire escape and watched the sunrise through the clouds and wondered whether Abel was doing the same.

I was a zombie in all my classes, and I did my best to avoid Trish, no longer feeling up to playing the game that was my life. It was no use, though, because she was unavoidable at home.

"What should I wear?" she asked me.

"For what?" I kept my eyes glued to my Kindle, as I desperately tried to escape reality.

She sighed dramatically as she stared at me. "For my date with Abel."

"You're still doing that? I thought you would have lost interest by now."

"Yeah, right. I need to hit that first. There's something about that guy…"

"I get it." I held up my hand to stop her from continuing. "Wear something tiny. Show him what he's missing." I wanted her to hurry up and get it over with so he wouldn't be at our apartment anymore. I wanted things to go back to our own fucked-up version of normal. I didn't like Abel stealing my dream time from Brock.

"That's a given. I'm thinking the black mini with that pink halter. Put my girls front and center." She grabbed her boobs, and I rolled my eyes.

"Sounds great. Whatever you think."

"Awesome! He's going to be here any minute."

"Wait…what?" I put down my Kindle and looked up at her.

"Change of plans. He called me last night. He's dying to get in this."

That son of a bitch. After his whole "I wish it was you" speech, he called Slutty McBoobs and moved up their fuckfest? Wow. This was just freaking amazing. I tossed my Kindle and got up from the couch, determined to prove I didn't care.

I stalked off to my closet and began to rip through my clothing, but nothing could compare to what Trish would have on. I ran out of my room and knocked on her door.

"Come in," she practically purred.

"Calm yourself. It's just me." I stepped inside her room. "I need to borrow some clothes. I'm going out."

"Really?" She jumped with excitement. "You have a date?" Why did she have to sound so surprised?

"Not yet, but I will before the night's over."

"That's my girl. Take what you want."

I made my way to her closet and dug through it, trying to find something sexy that still kept everything as covered as possible. I pulled out a deep-purple V-neck top and an off-white skirt that barely covered my ass if I stood perfectly straight.

I took off to my room and changed into my super-slut gear. I kept my hair down because I knew there wasn't much time. Instead I focused on my face. I gave myself smoky eyes and used three coats of mascara. This was as good as it was getting.

I hurried out of the bathroom and ran into a brick wall, better known as Abel. My eyes traveled up his body to his eyes; they were locked on my chest, which was pressed against him and pushing out of my top.

"My eyes are up here," I repeated his words from the other day with a confident smile. I wasn't going to let him know he bothered me.

"I know where they are, Delilah." His eyes lingered on my chest for an extra second before they met mine.

"Have fun on your date." I pulled out of his arms and walked around him to my room, letting out the breath I was holding as I stepped inside. The door closed behind me, and I whipped around to see Abel standing in my room in front of the closed door.

"Can I help you?" I asked with a cocky smirk as I tightened the back of one of my earrings. He walked closer.

"I had you all wrong, Kettle." His eyes traveled up and down my body. "You *are* just like us."

I knew he was trying to insult me, but I didn't care. "If you can't beat 'em…"

"…whore yourself out to the first willing drunk to prove a half-assed point?" he finished, and my eyes narrowed.

"Shut up."

He took a step closer, and I took one back. "Save yourself the cab fare, and let me take care of you right here."

"Fuck you," I spat as I shoved against his chest.

"Exactly." He pushed against my hands and closed the gap between us, letting me feel just how serious he was.

"Why are you acting like such an asshole?" I asked, as his face hovered over mine.

"This is who I am, right? This is what you want? You want to be treated like Trish? Like trash?"

"This outfit doesn't change who I am." I folded my arms over my chest, feeling stupid and childish.

"Remember that fact tonight when every prick in the club is trying to undress you on the dance floor because you're practically fucking naked. This…" He motioned to my clothing. "…doesn't make a fucking difference."

He turned and left my room, closing the door behind him. I stared at the wall in disbelief as I listened to Trish and Abel laugh and chat on their way out of the apartment, my heart shattering inside my chest.

A few minutes later, my phone chimed, and I picked it up and looked at the screen through blurry eyes.

I'm sorry.

That was all he said, but it didn't matter, and I didn't respond. I got up and pulled myself together for a night on the town. The cab arrived twenty minutes later, and I was off to Cloud Nine. I was sure Trish and Abel wouldn't be there because she hated the fact that the walls were purple. She thought it made her look orange with her fake tan.

I started the night by pounding back a few shots. My head began to swim, and my limbs became deliciously numb. The magic powder that was left in Trish's room added a nice touch, and soon I was flying. I was the life of the party.

I danced with anyone who was willing and screamed when a song came on that I loved. People bought me drinks left and right, and I couldn't believe I hadn't jumped in with both feet sooner. Trish lived like a goddess, and now I was on my own pedestal and never wanted to come down.

"You're so fucking sexy," the guy grinding against my ass moaned into my ear. I turned around to face him, blinking several times before I could focus on his face. He had dark hair and hadn't shaved for a few days, but through beer goggles, he was definitely doable.

"What's your name?" I asked, smiling brightly as my high grew.

"Who cares?"

Maybe I had no idea what I was doing. How fucking hard was it to get laid? "I'm going to get another drink."

He nodded and disappeared deeper into the crowd. I worked my way back to the bar as my phone vibrated. I pulled it out and moved it away from my face as my eyes struggled to focus on the small type.

How's the book?

I rolled my eyes and motioned for the bartender. "What can I get you, beautiful?" His eyes were fixed on my chest.

"Give me something hard," I yelled over the noise.

"Oh, darlin', I can give you something hard." His tongue ran over his lips, and I drew back in disgust. My phone vibrated again.

That good, huh?

I quickly typed a reply, not wanting to deal with Abel's shit.

Wouldn't know, but this bartender says he has something hard for me. ;)

"Just give me a double Jameson with a Coke back," I called out, and he nodded, looking unpleased. My phone lit up in rapid succession with messages.

Guess I did have you wrong.
You had me fooled.
Brock would be proud.

That last one gutted me, and I drank back my shot and stumbled toward the front door, wanting nothing more than to get away from everyone. I called a cab and sat on the curb as I waited for it to arrive and take me as far away from this place as I could get.

The trip was a blur, and my stomach swam with every dip and bump in the road. When the cab finally pulled over, I knew it was going to be a long night. I threw the driver a twenty and stumbled up to bed.

My eyes closed and begged the room to stand still as my phone vibrated.

Do I need to come find you?

"Stupid asshole," I slurred as I typed a message back to him.

I'm in bed.

I groaned as I rolled onto my back and looked up to the ceiling. Then Abel responded:

Whose bed?

My phone rang before I could send back a smartass response.
"Whose bed?" he asked angrily.
"What is your fucking deal?"
"You gonna answer the question?" I heard Trish in the background, but she didn't seem to be paying any attention to the phone call.

"My bed. You done?" I snapped, as I kicked off my shoes.

"Liar, liar, Kettle. I'm looking at your bed right now, and it's empty," he said in a hushed tone.

"Ugh. Get out of my room, and stop calling me 'Kettle'!"

"Are you alone?" he asked angrily. I rubbed my hand over my forehead, wanting to lie and tell him I was at some strange guy's house, but I couldn't do it.

"I'm alone. Now get out of my room."

"Fine. I'll go to *our* room," he said, and the call disconnected. Just fucking great. I rolled over and stared at the small dresser across the room in the spooky old house. I didn't know why I'd come here, but anything seemed better than listening to Trish and Abel screwing all night long.

I waited for the inevitable fight that was going to come. If I wasn't with someone, there was only one place I would be. It only took about ten minutes for me to hear his car pull up outside and the engine cut off. I listened to the car door open and slam. It was only one. He didn't bring Trish, and I thanked God for small miracles, but as the front door opened, my heart raced.

I listened to it close, and the lock clicked. Then I heard his heavy footsteps up the steps and down the hallway. I held my breath as the door opened; I was in no condition to fight, but I would give it all I had. I glanced at the silhouette of Abel in the doorway. He didn't move for a long moment, giving me time to fully regret every decision I'd made that night.

"What are you trying to prove?" he asked. The anger in his voice was gone, replaced with concern, and it somehow made me more uncomfortable.

I tried to respond, but a sob escaped my chest, and he crossed the room quickly and knelt beside the bed. His fingers ran over my forehead and through my hair as his eyes searched my face.

"I didn't think you'd be here, and I wanted one night of not having to listen to Trish getting laid. How did you know where to find me?"

"Lucky guess. If you wanted to avoid me, you shouldn't have come to my place," he said, as his fingers continued to soothe me.

"You *live* here?"

"Off and on. I bought it when my grandpa got sick. I knew I couldn't stay in his place after he died...so I wanted a place of my own, and I found this." He looked around the room. "It needed someone to take care of it, and I figured I could do the job."

"You have your hands full." I looked around the room and back at Abel, whose eyes never left mine.

"Don't I know it," he said with a sigh, and pushed himself to his feet as he shook his head. "Trish is pissed."

"Great." I put my hand over my eyes. "I can't deal with her right now."

"You don't have to." He pulled open a dresser drawer and tossed a T-shirt at me. "Put that on. I'm going to go get you a snack and some water." He walked toward the door but turned back to add, "Don't go fucking disappearing, Kettle. If I have to hunt you down again, I won't be so nice." He left, and I pulled off my shirt and skirt and slipped the T-shirt over my head. I reached my hands behind my back and unhooked my bra and pulled it off.

Chapter Eleven

Comfort Food

A few minutes later, Abel came back with a sandwich and a bottle of water. I ate the food with no complaint and guzzled half the water before coming up for air.

His eyes traveled down my bare legs and back to my face. "I'll sleep down on the couch. Yell if you need anything." He moved to get up from the edge of the bed, and I grabbed his wrist. He looked down at my fingers and back to me.

"Can you just stay until I fall asleep?"

"That's a bad idea." He shook his head, but I tightened my fingers as I silently pleaded with him not to leave me alone.

"Just talk to me," I said.

"We don't have anything to talk about." He shook his head. "What the hell am I going to do with you, Kettle?"

He stood, and I let my grip slip, but he didn't leave. I watched as he pulled his shirt over his head, and I saw every dip and rise of his muscles in the moonlight. He stared down at me as he let his shirt fall to the floor and crawled into bed next to me. I slid over the tiny twin bed, and he turned me so my back was facing his chest. His arm slid under my waist and the other over my hip as he pulled my body back against him.

"Thank you," I whispered, as he breathed over the back of my neck, sending a chill through my body.

"Thank me in the morning when you get out of here unscathed." His voice was deep and rough, like gravel.

I closed my eyes, knowing damn well sleep wouldn't come anytime soon. We lay in comfortable silence, and for once my heart raced due to something other than anxiety. It thumped as his heart drummed.

"Can I ask you something?" I held my breath as I waited for a response. I felt him nod, his head moving against my neck. "Why don't you just go back?"

"Nothing to go back to."

I nodded and curved my body into him more as his arms tightened a fraction. "Same here." I breathed deeply, and his arms clasped me more tightly before he relaxed his hold.

His lips moved against the side of my neck, causing my head to swim. "We both know that isn't true," he said.

If I had breathed, I wouldn't have heard him speak, but his words echoed in my chest, and guilt washed over me in heavy, drowning waves. I closed my eyes and hoped Brock didn't show his face in my dreams tonight. I couldn't look him in the eye. But I was never that lucky.

"Are you scared about leaving?" Brock's lips pressed against my temple, and I froze, wanting this moment to last forever.

"I don't know what to do without you." I grabbed my shirts from my drawer and shoved them into a plastic bag on my bed. With his fingers he brushed the hair over my shoulder, exposing my neck.

His hot lips pressed against my skin, and I sighed, loving how sweet he was to me.

"It's not forever," he told me. "I promise. My mom said I'll be out of here in a few weeks if I stay out of trouble."

I glanced at him, knowing it would take a miracle for him to stay out of trouble.

"I'll be good, Bird. I promise. I won't screw this up for us. You just have to get through a few weeks of school without me."

"I know. I'll be fine. I just can't imagine not having you wake me up every morning." I tried to sound optimistic, but it was hard when everything in my life had gone wrong. Brock's hand went to my cheek, and he turned my head to face him.

"One day I'll be there to wake you up again, Bird. I promise. We'll have our forever."

Strong hands held me tightly as I woke up to the first light of morning. I smiled as I stretched my aching muscles.

"I could wake up like this every day," Abel grumbled against my shoulder, and I squeezed my eyes closed as he awoke fully and his fingers slowly loosened their hold on me. "Delilah…" He said my name as if he were just realizing who he had spent the night with, ruining the perfect dream from the night before. I wondered how many different women had awoken in the same position as me and wished I'd spared myself the humiliation.

"Hoping for someone else?" I knew it was rude, but I'd be lying if I said I hadn't woken up expecting Brock.

"Definitely not." He rolled onto his back behind me, and I turned over onto my other side to face him. He reached down to the front of his jeans and readjusted himself. He certainly wasn't shy—not that he had any reason to be. His head turned toward me, and our noses nearly touched.

"Sleep well?" he asked with a devilish smirk, and I shrugged, completely drowning in the ocean of his eyes. "Sorry. It has a mind of its own."

I giggled and buried my face in the pillow between us, my hand covering my eyes. His fingers wrapped around mine, and he pulled my hand from my face, lacing our fingers.

"Are you embarrassed, Kettle?" He was making fun of me, and I scowled as I tried to free my hand from his.

"Don't be stupid. You're the one who should be embarrassed," I shot back.

He glanced his toward his crotch and back to me. "I haven't had any complaints."

"Doesn't count if they're too wasted to speak." I rolled onto my back and draped my arm across my forehead.

Abel propped himself on his side, and his eyes traveled the length of my body. "Got you in my bed, didn't I?"

"Dream on." I sat up and slid off the end of the bed, my sober mind catching up with how stupid I'd acted the night before.

Abel fell onto his back and watched me as I moved around the bedroom, collecting my clothing. "Thank you for taking care of me last night. I know I screwed up your plans."

"It's no big deal. There's always tonight."

"Shit! I'm late for class. What time is it?" I ignored his comment about Trish; it was easier to block out things than dwell on them.

Abel lifted his arm and looked at his watch. "It's time for an omelet."

I stood up and glared at him, my hands full of slut gear. "I have to go to class. We aren't all pissing in the wind and hoping life works out."

"Have you ever tried to piss in the wind, Kettle? People would pay good money—"

I put up my hands and shook my head. "What time is it?"

"Noon."

"Are you fucking kidding me?" I grabbed a pair of his basketball shorts off his dresser and pulled them on. I hurried out of the bedroom with Abel laughing as he followed a few steps behind.

"You might as well take the day off," he called after me, as I took off across the lawn to his car.

I jumped into the passenger seat and watched him as he strolled casually to the car, a shirt over his shoulder. He slid in and started the engine then flipped through the radio stations. He rolled down his window and grabbed a pack of cigarettes from the dash, popping one into his mouth and holding the pack out to me. I shook my head and watched as he patted his pockets for a lighter. "I think I left it in the house. Do you mind if I—"

"Ugh." I leaned forward and pushed in the built-in lighter.

"Very smart, Kettle. You don't need college after all." Abel put the car in drive and headed toward my place as I silently cursed him the entire trip.

The apartment was empty, because unlike me, Trish had made it to where she needed to be this morning. I took her clothes into my room and dropped them onto the dirty-laundry pile to wash later. Abel stood in my bedroom, leaning against the doorframe.

"I'll wash your clothes and get them back to you," I told him.

"Don't worry about it. If I ever need some, it'll be nice to have them here."

"I don't even want to know the situation that would require you to need an extra set of clothes while you're here."

His eyebrow lifted as he looked me over, and I realized how stupid my statement was.

"Well, at least if I hurry, I can still make my last class." I moved to walk out of the bedroom, but Abel didn't step out of the way.

"I clothe you and give you shelter, and you refuse to feed me. What would Jesus do, Kettle?"

"You're a bad influence."

"I've been called worse."

"Fine. I'll make you something to eat."

He stepped out of my way, and I went to the kitchen to get started. I pulled open the fridge and dug around for the eggs but found an empty carton. "The eggs are gone. What else do you like?" I called out, as I looked over my shoulder.

Abel stood just outside my room with a small black dress dangling from his finger. "I like this."

I walked over to him and snatched it from his hand. "Seriously. You need to learn boundaries." I tossed it onto the pile of clean clothes I'd ripped out of my closet the night before when trying to find something suitable for clubbing.

"Says the girl who slept in my bed last night."

"Do you want me to feed you or not?"

He nodded, and I walked back to the kitchen and resumed my place in front of the fridge as I searched for something that would take minimal effort to prepare. Abel groaned as he slid into the chair behind me. I pulled out the little bit of leftover spaghetti and held it up for his approval.

"Absolutely." He smiled, carefree, as he laced his hands behind his head. I uncovered the bowl and popped it into the microwave, pressing my back against the counter and drumming my fingers at my sides as I waited.

"Why Trish?" he asked, and my fingers stilled.

"I should ask you the same," I replied, but his gaze never wavered.

"She is who she is. No hidden agenda."

The microwave dinged, and I turned to grab our food and a couple of forks. I took the seat next to Abel and held out a fork. He took it with a smile, and we both ate in silence.

"After college are you moving back to Mississippi?"

"I have no idea where I'll be," I said, because it was the truth. "Who knows what'll happen tomorrow, let alone a few years from now?"

There was a bite left in the bowl, and he leaned back in his seat, letting me have it. Abel grabbed the bowl and took it to the sink to wash it out.

"So you and Trish are going out tonight?" I asked, and his hands were still for a moment before he rinsed out the bowl and placed it on a dish towel on the counter.

"That's the plan. You think you'll need to be rescued again?"

"I'm staying in tonight. I can only take so much humiliation." I pushed myself to my feet and headed into the bathroom to brush my teeth. Abel leaned against the doorframe as he watched me. I blinked as my reflection appeared to fade and blur before me. I rubbed the heel of my hand over my eye as I groaned.

"I'm never drinking again," I moaned, as I stuck my toothbrush in my mouth.

"You have an extra one of those?"

I pointed to the door below the sink and stepped out of the way as he pulled it open and grabbed an unopened toothbrush.

He didn't wait for me to finish as he began to brush his teeth, his large frame taking up all the room in front of the mirror. Toothpaste foamed over my lips, and I used my hand to keep it from dripping as I shoved against him with my hip. He grinned as he held his stance firmly, and I pushed all my weight into his side. He sighed dramatically and stepped out of my way. I bent over and spat, cupping water and using it to rinse my mouth. As I stood up and looked in the mirror, Abel was directly behind me, an entire head and shoulders taller than I was. He grinned, the toothbrush protruding from his mouth as he winked. I watched as my cheeks turned six shades of pink and wondered whether that was what I looked like every time he did something like that.

He tapped my shoulder, pulling me from my thoughts, and I stepped to the side so he could finish as I wiped my lips on a hand towel before heading into the living room. I plopped down on the end of the couch and clicked on the television with the remote. Abel came out of the bathroom and sat on the cushion beside me, thigh pressed to thigh, arm against arm.

"You know there's another cushion." I clicked through the channels.

"I like this one."

"Child."

"Play nice, Kettle."

I rolled my eyes and fought against the tug of my lips to smile. I clicked; Abel stretched. I clicked, and he slid farther down in his seat. I clicked, and he snatched the remote from my fingers and scrolled through the channels.

"I can't believe I skipped class to put up with this."

"Come on. You know this is much more fun."

Our eyes met, and I looked back at the television with an indifferent shrug. He settled on a movie called *Twelve* about a drug dealer.

"How appropriate," I snorted, and he gave me a sideways glance.

"I'll have you know this is a very deep movie about relationships and loss. Besides, you can't judge me after that smut you made me watch the other day."

"*Wild Things* isn't smut. It's a deep movie about relationships and loss." We both laughed, and Abel's hand fell on the bare skin of my thigh. My giggle died in my throat; I hated and loved having him so close.

"Do you like Trish?" I stared ahead at the movie as I bit my lower lip with my teeth.

"She's nice."

"Ha!"

"Come on," he said. "She isn't that bad. She's just looking for fun, nothing serious."

I knew he was right, but the thought of the two of them together didn't fit. It was like forcing two puzzle pieces together that clearly didn't belong because it was easier than looking for the right match.

"You're not jealous, are you, Lie?"

I glanced at Abel as I felt my cheeks burn under his gaze, and my heart hammered against the inside of my chest.

"You'll get to see Brock soon, and you'll get to go out and do all these things with him too."

I relaxed back in my seat and nodded. I was jealous, but for all of the wrong reasons, and my stomach twisted into knots. Abel's fingers patted my leg, and then they were gone. I pulled my knees to my chest and wrapped my arms around them as I tried to focus on the movie.

After about a half hour of not focusing on the film, I heard my phone ring from my bedroom. I hopped up, dashed to my room, and grabbed it from my dresser, cringing when I saw it was Marie.

"Hello?" I answered, as I stood in the hallway. Abel glanced at me for a second.

"You running again, Delilah?"

"Of course not." I tried not to sound defensive.

"I went out of my way to see you yesterday."

"I know you did. I'm sorry. I don't know what I was thinking."

Abel got up from the couch and walked by me into the kitchen. I watched as he pulled open the fridge and bent over. He had a cute butt.

"Did you hear me, Delilah?"

"I'm sorry. What?"

Abel looked over his shoulder and smirked before pulling out two sodas and holding them up. I nodded and looked away as I tried to focus on Marie.

"I won't be able to see you on Friday," she said. "My sister is getting married, and she wants me to help her pick out a dress."

"It's fine. It's whatever. I have plans Friday anyway. I was gonna tell you."

Abel cocked his head to the side as he popped open his soda and took a sip as he slowly walked toward me.

"I don't want to put you out," Marie said.

"It's fine. Really." I glanced away from Abel's questioning gaze.

Abel leaned in toward my free ear, his lips brushing over it and his breath tickling me as he whispered, "What are we doing Friday?"

I put my finger to my lips to tell him to be quiet and pushed back against his chest.

"Is that him?" he asked.

My eyes widened in warning. He took another drink as I smiled.

"You have company?" Marie asked. "Did I call at a bad time?"

"No. Just my roommate's boyfriend." I glared at him, and he headed into the living room and sat down on the center cushion then turned up the volume on the television. "I'll call you if I need you. I'm fine. I swear."

"All right. You have my number." She hung up, and I groaned. Marie was probably the most unprofessional therapist on the planet, but I liked that about her. She didn't have kids of her own, and she liked to mother me, which was kind of nice, even though it could be annoying as hell. I tossed my phone onto my bed then went to the living room and sat back down on the couch in the same spot I'd occupied before. Abel adjusted himself so that we were once again pressed side to side.

"He has trust issues, huh?"

"Huh?"

"I get it. If there was a guy like me walking around my girl's house, I probably would lose my mind too."

It sunk in that he thought I'd been talking to Brock, and I didn't correct him. What was I supposed to say? That my overbearing therapist likes to call me randomly and tell me about her life?

"And what kind of guy is that?"

Abel ignored me as he picked up the remote and flipped through the movie channels. He stopped on a scary movie that was showing a man getting stabbed in the shoulder as blood sprayed across the screen. I cringed and curled closer into his side.

"You scared?" He smirked as his arm went over my shoulders.

"I'm not a fan of violence." I tried to focus on the television and not the places where our bodies touched; the closeness sent waves of heat through his shirt, which I still wore.

"Aw…I won't let them come through the screen and get you," he replied sarcastically, and I smacked him lightly on the chest as I settled into his side. The killer wiped the blood from his blade on his shirt and set off toward a home in the woods that vaguely reminded me of Abel's work in progress. He was met by three guys in varsity jackets who challenged him to a fight in their inebriated state. I turned my head, hiding my face against Abel's neck, my knees turned to the side on his lap.

"What's happening?" I asked, as I breathed in the scent of his Polo Sport.

"Jock number one took a knife to the jugular," he said with a laugh, as his free hand fell on my bare knee on his lap. "Number two is putting up a fight, but he's doing it all wrong. He's…aw… come on."

"What happened?"

"I think he just lost his football scholarship. Number three swung and missed. He's trying to run. Ohhh!" He yelled, causing me to jump. "He didn't make it." His thumb tapped against my skin, and my heart beat in time with his absent-minded touch.

"Can I look?" I started to turn my head, but Abel's fingers came up and turned my cheek back into the crook of his neck.

"I don't think you want to see this part."

"Why? What's going on?"

Abel cleared his throat and adjusted in his seat as his hand went back to my leg. "He's gonna kill a couple on the couch."

"What's happening?" I asked, and I felt his body shiver slightly as my breath blew over his neck.

"They're making out." His voice was a quiet whisper as I felt his pulse increase under my fingertips. "He's…" He cleared his throat. "Sliding his hand up her thigh." His thumb glided lightly back and forth over the inside of my knee. "The killer is watching from inside the doorway. Her eyes are closed, and the guy's slipping his hand under her skirt." His face moved a fraction of an inch until our cheeks were pressed against each other's and his hot breath blew over my ear. I heard the panting and the quiet moans from the movie, and I contemplated turning to watch, but I was frozen against Abel, oddly enjoying his play by play of the scene and not sure seeing it for myself would do anything to make this situation any less intense. "She likes it," he whispered.

"Yeah?" I whispered back, my voice coming out breathy.

"Yeah." His fingers gripped my lower thigh more tightly.

"What are they doing now?" I asked, as my hand slid up from his chest to the side of his neck.

"He's kissing her." His face pulled back an inch, putting our mouths closer to each other. "She's moving against his hand." He swallowed hard, and I stayed pinned against him, motionless, as I listened to the sounds of lovemaking, their moans deafening in the small space. "He's taking off her panties and sliding them down her legs."

My eyes closed as I was entranced by his voice, my mouth suddenly dry. I heard the clicking of the remote as Abel turned down the volume just as the female became more vocal in her pleasure. Abel's hand slid a few inches up my thigh to the edge of the shorts I was wearing. "She's spreading her legs for him, and he's sliding between them. Her hands are undoing his jeans."

My breathing grew ragged, and my fingers gripped his shirt collar. "Yeah?"

"Yeah…" His face angled toward mine, and his breath blew over my lips as our foreheads pressed against each other's. His hand slipped up and down the outside of my thigh, sending tingles vibrating through my skin with each pass. "And now he's sliding into her."

"You're not even looking at the screen," I said with a laugh, and my eyes opened as I glanced at the television. The movie was rolling the credits, and I pushed against Abel's chest to back him away from me as my cheeks burned with embarrassment. "You're such a liar!"

"You were enjoying yourself. I didn't want to disappoint you," he joked, and smacked his chest.

"You asshole! You didn't have to make fun of me!"

Abel looked at me. His eyes started on my thighs, glided over my chest, and traveled up to meet my gaze. "You really are naïve, Kettle. I should go." He motioned to stand, and I grabbed his arm to keep him from getting up.

"Don't do that."

"Do what?"

"Look down at me like Trish does," I said. "Neither of you knows the first damn thing about me. I didn't grow up in a fucking bubble, and my life wasn't sailboats and designer drugs like you two. *You're* the ones who are naïve. You like to party every day and fuck a new stranger each night like you're so badass. You don't have the first clue."

"You think you're badass, Lie?" Abel leaned closer until I smelled the minty toothpaste on his breath. I refused to move away because I knew that was exactly what he expected me to do. "You want to know what it's like to be on a sailboat with *me*?" He smirked, but it wasn't playful, and his voice was low and menacing. "This…" He pulled up his shirt to show me the hot-white scar over his ribcage. "This is from the last time I was on a boat—me, my mom, my dad. I was the only one who came back home that day; only home was gone for me. My whole world was gone, so yeah, I can teach you about sailboats and drugs and fucking some random stranger just to feel something—anything other than emptiness. I can show you all that, *little girl*."

I leaned away from him, stunned into silence by his confession and mortified that I'd brought up such a painful memory for him.

"I-I'm so sorry, Abel. I didn't have any idea."

"That's right. You have *no* idea." He stood and looked down over me with what could be described only as disgust as he headed for the front door. He yanked it open, and it slammed against the wall before banging shut behind him.

Chapter Twelve

Anarchy

I stared at the television as tears formed in my eyes and spilled down my cheeks. I sat like that until the credits rolled during the next movie and my eyes ran dry. I took a scalding-hot shower to remove any remnants of Abel's touch. I was pulling on sweatpants and Brock's anarchy T-shirt, which always made me feel a little closer to him.

Trish had come home and locked herself in her room, which was fine by me because I wasn't in the mood to talk. I knew I should call Marie. She would answer on the first ring and wouldn't judge me, but I didn't care anymore.

The wall had gone back up, and I no longer gave a fuck about anything. It hurt less that way. I was used to being pushed around and knocked down, but now I had become the bully. I'd played my part too well and hurt one of the few people who saw the real me.

The world continued to spin; the clock ticked; and life moved forward with no destination or goal. As I sat down at the kitchen table and ate a bowl of cereal, Trish finally emerged from her room, looking stunning as usual in a pale-yellow sundress that dipped dangerously low on her chest and fell just below her ass. Her mile-high strappy sandals made her look like a supermodel ready for the runway.

"What happened to you?" she asked, as she looked over my damp and tangled hair, my face makeup free and puffy from crying. "Guy trouble?"

I glanced up at her, debating whether to give her the usual canned sarcastic response or open up and offer her a sliver of truth. I didn't have time to decide, because a knock came at the door.

"Speaking of trouble," she called out in a singsong voice as she went to open the door.

"You look incredible," Abel said from the hallway, and Trish giggled. "Good enough to eat."

I nearly chocked on my Cocoa Puffs.

"I just have to grab my purse," she replied then headed to her room as Abel stepped into view, his hands shoved into his jeans pockets. His eyes were glazed over and red, which only made their blue-green color stand out more.

He looked past me, as if I weren't even there, and smiled broadly as Trish reemerged. His hand slid to the back of her neck, and he pulled her lips to his. I could only stare as they made out a few feet away from me.

"Don't wait up," Trish called out, and wiped her finger under her lower lip to make sure her lip gloss wasn't smeared. She took Abel by the hand and pulled him toward the door. As soon as they were gone, I dropped my spoon, my appetite ruined.

The world spun.

The clock ticked.

Life moved forward.

The only problem was that I was stuck in the past. I refused to let myself move forward and live. I survived, and right now that was all I could do.

I went to my room and grabbed my Kindle and read until my eyes went unfocused; I checked the clock every few minutes. By four in the morning, I debated going grocery shopping. I was craving an omelet. I settled for a quick walk to the convenience store and picked up some breakfast supplies. By the time I got back to the house, my appetite had vanished.

Around five I decided to lie on my bed in the dark and find shapes in the plaster smudges in the ceiling.

A bang and shuffle, bang and shuffle came from the front door.

"Shh. You're going to wake up Lie," Trish whispered with a laugh.

"She's a big girl. She'll get over it," Abel panted, and it sounded as if they were making out and tripping their way to Trish's room. I heard the distinct sound of a zipper coming down and a thud as Abel's back hit the wall across the hall from my room. I pushed up on my elbows as glassy, empty eyes stared back at me through the open door to my bedroom. My gaze traveled lower to his hand, which was tangled in Trish's blond hair as she knelt in front of him.

I rolled over and covered my face with my pillow as fresh tears pricked my eyes. Abel muttered something, but it was muffled by my pillow, and the noises stopped with the clicking of Trish's bedroom door.

My thoughts were a scrambled mess of memories from the past and present. I tossed and turned until the sun splashed lines of light through the blinds.

I got up and got ready for class, tiptoeing through the hall so I wouldn't wake anyone, but as I stepped out of the bathroom, Abel was waiting outside the door. I stared at the floor between us and stepped around him as he went inside.

I left through the front door before he came back out. Campus was two blocks to the left and three down. I enjoyed the walk on most days because it gave me time to think, but this morning I wanted to shut everything out.

I had only one class with Trish, and that was on Thursdays, so I knew I could avoid the horrid details of her night with Abel for at least a few hours. It didn't make a difference, though, because my brain zeroed in and focused on what could have happened, and that was probably much worse than the reality of the situation.

I felt bad for what I'd said to Abel that had sparked his memory of the death of his parents. That was what bothered me so much. That was what I told myself as I picked at my burger from the Stop Shop, delaying the inevitable trip home. All my worrying was for nothing as the apartment sat empty when I arrived.

I decided to make the best of my alone time and wash the dirty laundry. I was folding it and putting it away when the front door finally opened.

Trish arrived with Abel, Adam, and Sean. They were in mid-conversation as they entered, and I turned my back to my door as I continued to organize my laundry. The guys made their way to the living room, and Trish stopped at my room.

"Huge party at Sigma Chi tonight. Wear blue."

"Oh, I don't really feel like going." I shook my head and didn't turn around to look at her.

"Don't be such a pussy, Lie." After a moment she sighed. "Boy trouble?"

I nodded but didn't elaborate, and she left me alone and returned to the living room.

I headed to the kitchen and grabbed a soda. When I turned around, Abel was behind me, his hands shoved into his pockets.

"You really not going?"

"I don't want to go where I'm not wanted." I stepped around him, but he grabbed my arm, and we stood side by side.

"Who said you're not wanted?" he said quietly into my ear, and I immediately was taken back to our private moment on the couch. I chanced a glance at his eyes, and my chest tightened.

"I'm sorry about what I said."

He stood upright and released my arm, his snarky persona back with a flash. "Trish wouldn't say no to a party."

Hot and cold. Those were the two temperatures of Abel. There was no in-between. I felt like a complete ass as he left me standing in the kitchen alone, my apology still hanging, unaccepted, in the air.

"Is she coming?" Trish asked, as I stepped into the hallway.

"She'll come," Abel replied, as she squealed and wrapped her arms around his neck. I slipped into my room and dug out my navy-blue tank top and cut-off shorts. I planned to at least be comfortable if I was going to spend the night feeling miserable.

We took Abel's car, and he didn't hesitate to motion me into the backseat between Dumb and Dumber. Trish pushed herself against Abel's side, and his arm hung around her, his fingertips in front of my face as they drew small circles on her bare shoulder. Sean leaned forward so he could talk to Adam around me, and I pressed myself into the back of the seat to stay out of their conversation. Every once in a while, Abel chimed in or nodded as they talked about everything from sports to drugs.

The song "Brown Eyed Girl" came on the radio, and Abel turned it up. I saw him smirk, but he didn't look back at me while it played. It reminded me of my mother and what I'd told him she'd said about my eyes. It was a dig, and one I deserved, but it still hurt. I didn't belong here, and we both knew it.

We pulled up outside the frat house, and it was complete chaos. People were everywhere, and the anarchy didn't stop on the lawn. The entire house was wall-to-wall bodies. Trish bee-lined to the kitchen to get us some drinks. Abel poured shots for each of us and warned us not to take drinks from anyone but him. I rolled my eyes and was met with a glare as he held my cup inches from my hand.

"I get it," I snapped, and he finally handed me my drink. I gulped it down greedily and held it back to him for a refill. I tried to ignore the nagging memory of Brock's sister, Laurie, who'd been drugged at a similar party. I didn't need to be told about the conse-quences of trusting strangers. Brock had learned the hard way when his sister had died, and the butterfly effect from that event had destroyed my own life. Abel was about a year too late to save me.

"That's my girl!" Trish hollered as Abel poured. He tipped the bottle to his lips and took a long drink. His free hand rubbed up and down her back.

"Come on." Trish grabbed my wrist. "Let's go find you some guy and make that asshole of yours regret breaking your heart."

I looked at Abel as I replied while Trish pulled me away. "I'm a big girl. I'll get over it," I said, echoing his words from the night before. His jaw clenched, and the muscles jumped and pulled under his tanned skin.

"That's the fucking spirit. Tell me which one you think is cute because it's like a buffet up in this bitch."

I glanced around the room. "Which ones haven't you slept with?" I asked, as I raised an eyebrow.

Trish playfully smacked my arm. "We may have to go to a different college for that," she joked, and I began to relax as my veins warmed from the alcohol.

"That guy's cute." I gestured with my chin to a guy who was leaning over a coffee table, rolling dice.

"He's a douche. Stay away from him," Abel said into my ear from behind me. His body was pressed against mine for a moment before he stepped around me and handed Trish a cup.

"Funny coming from you, Pot. Most guys are douches. Some are just easier to tolerate." I laughed, and Trish joined in, but Abel was less than amused.

"How would you even know? Oh...that's right. You're a badass. How could I forget?"

Ouch. We were back to the jokes that I was a virgin. Fucking awesome. I took the cup from Trish's hand and drank down some liquid courage before handing it back to her. "Only one way to find out," I said with a wink, as Trish grinned widely.

I walked over to the coffee table and watched for a moment as the guys took turns rolling the dice and yelled each time they stopped.

"Looks fun," I hollered over the music, and the hot guy looked up and nodded. His eyes traveled down my body and back up with a smile.

"Want to play?" His dark hair hung over his eyes, but he kept it swept to the side. His arms were thick and muscular, and I imagined he was a football player or something equally as physical.

"I think I'll just watch for a bit."

"You want a drink or something?" he asked.

I knew better. I knew Brock would be absolutely livid. But he wasn't here. He broke his promise of forever. I glanced over my shoulder at Trish, avoiding Abel as I looked back to mystery guy and nodded.

"I'm Delilah."

"Hey, there, Delilah." He laughed as he sang the song title, and I fought against rolling my eyes. He *was* kind of a douche. "I'm James."

"Nice to meet you."

"I'll go grab that drink. Wait here."

"OK," I whispered, as he set off toward the kitchen, and I was left awkwardly watching a bunch of drunken strangers play dice. Trish dragged Abel over, and her eyes were lit up like she had just spotted some unattended drugs.

"So?" she asked.

"He seems nice." I nodded. "He went to get me a drink."

"He's a gentleman!" she squealed.

"You've got to be fucking kidding me." Abel glared down at me.

"What?" Trish and I asked in unison.

"You're going to let some strange guy pour your drink?"

"He's not strange. He's nice," I replied defensively. I knew I was being stupid, but I was tired of everyone telling me what was best for me.

"Every guy is nice when he's trying to fuck you," Abel sneered. My smile fell, and I felt everyone turn to listen to our conversation. "God, you're like a fucking child. Do I really need to baby-sit you again?"

James appeared at my side as he looked back and forth between Abel and me with a plastic cup in his hand. "You all right?" he asked, and Abel took the cup from him and placed it on the coffee table.

"She's fine. This conversation doesn't concern you."

"I was asking Delilah." James didn't back down from Abel's menacing tone, but he didn't look at him either. He kept his eyes locked on mine for an answer.

"You all right, *Delilah*?" Abel said my name as if it were a curse word, and I flinched, feeling like I'd been physically hit. "Tell you what." He turned to look at James as he picked up the cup. "Why don't you drink this, James?"

"I got my own, man. What's your fucking problem?"

Abel's eyes met mine, a faint smile on his lips, as if he had proven his point. "What's my problem?" He repeated the words as his eyes searched mine.

"I'm fine. I have to go. You're welcome to join me, James." I looked at Trish, who seemed completely confused, then up to Abel, who was ready for a fight. I shoved past him and worked my way toward the front door with James trailing behind me. I was out in the warm night air before the sadness rose, and I wished I hadn't told James to follow me.

"What the hell was that?" he asked, as he pointed over his shoulder to the house.

"Just a…misunderstanding." I shook my head as I ran my hand over my forehead. "Can you take me home?"

"Of course." He smirked, and my stomach turned.

James pulled a set of keys from his pocket and hit a button on the key chain. A car across the street beeped, and the lights flashed, signaling it was now unlocked.

I crossed the street and didn't give a second thought to slipping into the passenger seat. Abel appeared on the porch of the house, and when he saw us, he ran across the road.

"I just want to go to my place," I told James, who still had his door open. "Alone."

"Oh, come on, baby. The night is young."

"Get out of the fucking car, Lie." Abel was next to James's door, his jaw clenched in anger.

"She wants to go home with me, bro. Better luck next time," James shot back, but Abel ignored him, glancing around his side to see my face.

"Is this really what you want?" Abel asked, and I glanced at James. I sat back in my seat and turned to look out the front window.

"Take me home, James."

"Don't worry, man. I'll call you later." James closed the door, and his comment didn't make any sense. I turned to him, confusion written on my face as he flipped through his keys.

"What do you mean 'call him later'? You know him?"

James laughed and shook his head as he stuck the key in the ignition. "Everyone knows Abel."

It dawned on me that James probably was referring to buying drugs from him, and I'd wished I hadn't been so fucking stubborn and had listened for once. As the headlights came on and illuminated Abel, my eyes were drawn to the shiny metal object in his right hand.

"Fuck. Who are you to him?" James asked nervously. I glanced at him, unable to form words as his door was pulled open and he was ripped from his seat. Abel shoved him against the frame of the door, the gun pressed into the underside of his chin.

"I'm only going to say this once. If you ever come near Delilah again, I'll make the beating you took over Becca look like a fucking birthday party."

The memories of my past flooded my mind, leaving me paralyzed in fear.

"I won't come near her, man. Fuck." James raised his hands in surrender, and Abel gripped the collar of his shirt. Abel shoved him hard against the car and rounded the car to my side. He yanked open my door and held out his hand to me.

"Let's go, Kettle. I'm not asking you this time."

My gaze fell to the gun in his hand, and I couldn't breathe. My lungs felt like they were being squeezed in my chest. Abel's eyes followed mine, and he tucked the gun into the front of his jeans.

"I'm not going to hurt you, Lie. You can trust me," he said, as he pulled his shirt over the weapon, hiding it from view.

"I'm not going to make that mistake twice." I cowered away from him, and he took a step back as he ran his hand over his hair.

"I couldn't let you leave with him. You don't know what kind of person he is."

"But *you* do, don't you?" I swallowed the lump in my throat. "Because you're just like him." I glanced up in time to see his expression soften, replaced by regret.

"I was trying to *protect* you."

"Let me save you the trouble of history repeating itself. I'm not worth it." I stood, and he took a step back, looking as confused as I felt. I started to walk toward my apartment, no longer caring what might be lurking in the shadows.

I was two blocks away from the party when my phone rang. I ignored it and kept walking as fast as I could. Two blocks farther, and my phone had rung no less than three times and vibrated half a dozen. I crossed the street and dipped down an alley just to be sure that if anyone came looking for me, they wouldn't find me. I needed some time to myself as I sank into my memories.

Going back to school after I had run away only seemed to amplify my loser status. I didn't fit in with anyone, and I gave up trying.

I skipped school on most days, but the hunger pains began to outweigh the sadness, and I was forced to show my face just so I could have lunch. I sat in the far corner of the cafeteria with the other kids who were deemed too uncool to be seen with.

I took a bite of my Mexican pizza and dropped it onto my tray, careful not to look up from the table. Making eye contact with any of the other students was an invitation to start trouble in their eyes. Today I didn't need to, though, because they sought me out.

"Do you try to look hideous on purpose, or were you born that ugly?" Shelly said, as she stood on the opposite side of the table. I didn't look up, and she grew more frustrated with my lack of a response. "I asked you a question, freak."

I wiped the crumbs from my hands and took a deep breath as I finally met her glare. She pushed her long blond hair over her shoulder and smirked.

"What's your problem with me?" My voice was shaky, and I cleared my throat.

"My problem? I have to look at your stupid face every day. How am I supposed to keep my lunch down with your stupid face right here?"

I felt everyone's eyes on me as Shelly's voice grew louder. If I didn't leave now, I'd cry, and that would give them more ammunition. I pushed myself up from my seat and grabbed my tray. "I'm done now," I told her, "so you can go back to eating."

Shelly laughed as two girls appeared at her side and joined in.

"You know…" She placed her hands on the table and leaned in closer to me. "You could spare us all and just kill yourself. It's not like anyone wants you here."

"Her own stupid mom doesn't even want her," Keri added, and I felt like I was going to be physically ill.

I looked to the boy who sat in front of me. He was eating his food as if he were oblivious to the torture I was enduring. Even he knew I wasn't worth standing up for.

"Maybe I'll do that." I grabbed my tray and hurried to the trashcans by the door, where I dumped my food and dashed into the hall. My feet picked up pace when I was out of sight from the bullies, and I ran toward the emergency exit at the end of the hall, desperate to get outside before I began to sob.

It took only another ten minutes to reach my apartment, and I was thankful Abel's car wasn't out front. I stomped up the steps and into my room, anger flowing from every pore. I wanted to break something; I wanted to show everyone I wasn't a fucking kid, but I barely owned anything, and what little I did I couldn't part with. My phone rang again, and I answered it, ready to snap.

"What?" I yelled, as I slammed my bedroom door behind me and paced toward the living room.

"Are you home?" Abel sounded just as angry.

"Fuck you." I hung up, and the rang again before I could slip it into my pocket.

"Are. You. Home?" He paused between each word, and I knew he was trying to keep his cool.

"Oh, you want to come save me now? Is this the game you're playing? You can't be both the hero and the villain."

"Unlock the door."

I glanced toward the front door, and my heart jumped in my chest. I knew I should run up to it and turn the deadbolt, but my feet didn't move. "It's unlocked."

The line went dead, and a few moments later, Abel walked through and straight down the hallway toward me.

"What are you trying to prove?" I asked him. "I'm not as cool as you? I'm not as pretty as Trish? I fucking get it. I get it. You can stop now."

He stepped right in front of me, and I had to bend my neck to look up at him. "You want to get raped at a fucking party to prove you're popular?"

"You had *no* right to talk to me that way. What I do is none of your fucking business!" I poked my finger into his chest, and he wrapped his hand around my wrist, jerking it away to stop me.

"Is it Brock's business? Were you thinking about *him* at all while you were busy trying to become a statistic?" His grip on my wrist tightened.

"What the fuck do you care?"

"I don't give a shit about your stupid little boyfriend who won't even get on a fucking plane to come see you. I don't want you to get hurt just because you're mad at me."

"I'm not mad at you, Abel. That's where you're wrong. I don't give a *fuck* about you." I pushed against him with my other hand, and he stood there, unmoving.

"Really?"

"Yeah, really." I pushed again, and he took a step forward.

"You didn't give a fuck when I held you all night and you cried over Brock?" His voice was quiet and almost sweet. *Almost.*

"No." I glared at him as I shoved. He took another step forward, and I stepped back again, my body pressed against the wall.

"Not when we were on the couch together, Kettle?" His nose skimmed along my cheek as he inhaled.

"Shut up."

He grabbed my other wrist from his chest and held my hands beside me as he took one last step, his body flush against mine. "You don't feel anything?" he asked, his forehead against mine, his eyes closed. Our breathing was out of control from the anger and sexual tension that swirled in the air. "What about…" His lips moved to my ear. "…when I fucked your only friend in the room right next to you? What did you feel then?"

"I hate you." I used my body to push him away from me, and he stepped back with a light, sardonic laugh. I ran to my bedroom and slammed the door closed as I broke down, finally unable to hold back everything I'd been feeling since the day I'd lost Brock.

"Good. I'll stop wasting my fucking time," he yelled, as the front door slammed behind him.

Chapter Thirteen

Running

It didn't escape me that Trish never bothered to come see if I was OK. It wasn't something I'd ever expect of her, but on top of the pain that settled in my chest, it made it impossible to breathe.

I began to gather my things, throwing them haphazardly around the room through blurred vision. I wouldn't be here when she finally showed up, and I damn sure didn't want to face Abel again.

I shoved a few outfits into an old suitcase and made my way down the flight of steps on shaky legs. As I reached the curb, I pulled out my cell phone and called Uncle Greg. It took a few tries, but he finally answered.

"What happened?" he asked, his voice laced with sleep and concern. He coughed and wheezed as I waited patiently to respond.

"Nothing. I just need to get away for a few days."

He cleared his throat. "What about school?"

"I can drive one of your cars there."

He sighed loudly. "Why don't you use some of that money to get yourself something dependable? There's more than enough."

"I will. I just…Can I come for a few days?" I didn't want to think about the money Greg had given me when I moved out here. He already had done too much to help me.

"I'll leave the light on. Delilah, you know you never have to ask. This is your home now too."

"It's just for a little while." I hung up the phone and hailed a cab to take me to my uncle's place. It was larger than any one person could ever need. He had told me I was welcome to stay with him until I graduated from college, but I wanted to be on my own, away from anything connected to my past.

I slipped inside the front door of the massive two-story house, careful not to wake him as he snored on the recliner in front of the television, and made my way to my room. The house had minimal decorations, because Uncle Greg was a perpetual bachelor and thought knickknacks and paintings were clutter. My room was just at the top of the stairs, and I sighed as I pushed open the door. I didn't bother turning on the light because the moon shone brightly through the double doors that led to my balcony. Boxes of memories I had no intention of ever revisiting lined the left wall, but my uncle refused to throw them away. He insisted that one day I would regret tossing it all away, but all they did was remind me of the painful events that had brought me here. Still it warmed my heart that he had gone through the trouble of having my things sent here. It was nice to have someone who cared about my life.

I fell onto my California-king-size bed and stared at the ceiling fan until my heart rate slowed enough to allow me to get some rest.

"What do you think you're doing?" My mom had her hands on her hips as she stood at my bedroom door. Her hair was dark like mine, but she rarely wore it down or took the time to make herself look presentable anymore. Although she was younger than the other moms, her skin was beginning to wrinkle from her two-pack-a-day smoking habit. A cigarette dangled between her lips at this moment, and smoke drifted into my bedroom.

"I can't stay here anymore." I turned back to my bed, where I had gathered a few items and was shoving them into a tote bag.

"You run away again, you can bet your ass you're going right back to that shelter."

My heart raced at the thought of going back to Brock, but I knew he'd be out any day now, and I'd just be alone again.

"No one wants me here. Not even you. What's the point of forcing me to stay here and suffer?" I used the sleeve of my hoodie to wipe my tears as I continued to shove clothing into my bag.

"Who do you think you are, smartin' off to me like that, girl? You got a lot of nerve."

I turned around, and my mother was pointing at me with the two fingers that held her cigarette, her eyes narrowed in anger. "I don't think I'm anyone, Mom. That's the point. I'm a nobody. I just want to leave." I was practically hysterical and couldn't take much more of this. Any of it. Shelly was right; I should just end my suffering now.

"The seed of sin. Nothing good can come from that."

I fell onto my bed, my legs unable to support me under the weight of her words. I covered my face with my hands as sobs racked my body.

"Why can't you just love me? What did I ever do to you?" I knew better than to try to have any kind of meaningful conversation with my mom. I saw the nearly empty bottle of Jack Daniel's on the kitchen table. But I needed her now, and I was desperate.

"You were born." Her voice was cold, and there was no emotion in her words. She simply closed my door, and I was left alone with my pain.

I had hit a wall in my life, and at only seventeen years old, I didn't see any point in looking forward to tomorrow. I cried until the tears stopped coming, until my thoughts were a jumbled mess of sadness and regrets.

A knock came at my door, and I didn't bother to respond. After another knock, my mom opened it, not bothering with an invitation.

"You have a phone call."

I looked at her with confusion. No one ever called me. No one even had my number except...I jumped from my bed and shoved by her in the narrow doorway. I grabbed the phone from the kitchen counter, my lower lipped pulled between my teeth as I held the receiver midair, scared to find out who was on the other end. I couldn't handle any more disappointment.

"This is the first and last time a boy calls this house, you hear me? Last thing we need is another unwanted kid around here," she slurred, and my heart was in my throat as I pulled the phone to my ear.

"Hello?" I asked, and a breathy sigh came through the other end.

"I've missed your voice, Bird."

"Brock? Where are you? Are you out?" I looked around the room as if he'd suddenly manifest in the kitchen.

"Yeah. My mom picked me up this morning. I've been dying to call you for hours. I miss you."

"I miss you so much. You have no idea." I squeezed my eyes closed as I forced back the sadness that had plagued me all day. I twisted the phone cord around my fingers.

"I need to see you, Bird. I can't take being out without you."

"Same here, but my mom would flip if she found out I was gone." I glanced behind me to make sure she wasn't listening. When I was certain she had retreated to her bedroom, I couldn't help smile.

"I have to see you tonight," Brock said.

I ran my hand through my hair, knowing I should say no, but I couldn't. "OK."

"Where?"

"How far are you from the Piggly Wiggly?" I glanced over my shoulder again, but I was in no danger of my mother coming back out tonight. She was probably out cold.

He laughed. "That grocery store?"

"Don't make fun of the pig, city boy."

"I can be there in ten minutes. My parents went to bed an hour ago."

"I'll ride my bike over. Meet me where they keep the extra buggies off to the side."

"Bird, you're killing me. What the hell is a buggy?"

"The shopping carts."

"I'm sorry, but it's like you're speaking a whole different language down here." He laughed into the phone, and I pictured him shaking his head.

"You can pick on me once we're together," I told him. "I'm gonna leave now."

"See you there."

I hung up the phone and hurried into my bedroom to grab my sneakers. Then I slid out the door, putting them on at the top of the steps before making my way out of the apartment building. My bike was leaning against a wall, and I pushed up the kickstand, hopping on as I pushed the bike forward, anxious to get to Brock.

My feet couldn't pedal fast enough, and even though the store was right down the road, it felt like a million miles stood between us. The parking lot was empty; I was glad I wouldn't have to worry about running into anyone from school.

I leaned my bike against the building and looked around for Brock. Only a couple of minutes passed before I saw him walk across the parking lot in his anarchy shirt and dark jeans. I couldn't help laugh out of sheer happiness when he picked up his pace, and soon his arms were wrapped around me as he squeezed me painfully tight. Gone was the nasty soap smell from the shelter. I inhaled deeply, breathing in Curve Chill cologne and a wintergreen scent.

"Jesus, Bird. I've missed you so much. These last few weeks were hell." He pulled back to look at me. Suddenly his smile faded, and his eyebrows pulled together.

"What?" I asked, as his hands went to my cheeks.

"What happened? Why were you crying?"

"I wasn't. I'm fine." I was in such a hurry to meet him that I didn't even glance in a mirror. My eyes were probably puffy, and no doubt my skin was pink from all the tears I'd cried. I tried to look away, but he held me still.

"Don't do that. You can tell me what's wrong." His thumbs slid over my cheeks softly as his eyes searched mine.

"Things at school have gotten worse. It's fine. I'm fine now. It was just a bad day."

"Tell me what happened."

"I will...I promise. But can't we just be happy that we're finally together?"

Smiling, he pulled my face to his. When his lips pressed against mine, I felt all the tension from the day leave my body. His tongue ran over my upper lip, and I let my mouth open slightly to deepen our kiss.

"Is there somewhere we can go around here?" he asked, his forehead against mine.

"There's a place by the creek where I go when I want to be alone."

Brock nodded, and I reluctantly stepped away from him to grab my bike. We walked quietly across the parking lot in the direction of my apartment building, as I thought about spending time alone with him for the first time. I was nervous, but I'd never felt safer with anyone in my life.

"Bird, there's something we need to talk about."

"What?" I looked at him, but he stared at the road as we continued to walk.

"I might not be able to take you to Boston."

"What? Why not?" My heart lodged in my throat, and I prayed he wasn't going to break up with me.

"It would take weeks to come up with some money, and my parents want to send me to this boot-camp thing."

"What? They can't do that. You're going to be eighteen soon. They can't make you go there." I was panicking.

"Not for another five months, and they want me gone by next week. There's nothing I can do. I can't run away with you and risk us getting stranded, and until my birthday, they can do whatever the fuck they want." Brock shook his head as we slipped behind a row of houses into the trees. I propped my bike against one, and we continued toward the creek.

"I can't make it another five months, Brock. I can't. This place is killing me."

He grabbed my hand and laced our fingers together. We approached the edge of the water, where the grass grew thick and lush. He stopped and turned me toward him. "Tonight it's just us." His hand slid into my hair. "We'll worry about the rest tomorrow, but please...I just need tonight."

I nodded, and his lips crashed against mine. There was a hunger, a desperation in his touch. I tried to push the thought of losing him out of my mind. My hands slid up his chest and over his shoulders. His fingers tightened in my hair as his other hand slid over my hip and held my body against his.

"I don't know what I'll do without you," he mumbled breathlessly against my lips as his hand slid up my side, dragging my tank top up. His fingers glided over my stomach and along the waistband of my jeans. His gaze dropped between us before his eyes searched mine. I pulled my lip between my teeth as I nodded, and his lips were on mine again.

We sunk to the grass, and Brock pulled his shirt over his head and placed it on the ground before lowering me onto it, his body on top of mine. The moonlight filtered through the trees, and as the wind blew, it sent spots of light dancing over us. I slid my hands over his back as his hands went under my shirt and his palm moved over my breast. His lips traveled to my neck as he trailed kisses down to my collarbone.

He pulled back, his eyes on mine, and I smiled. "You sure about this, Bird?" he asked.

"You're the only thing I'm sure about."

He grabbed my shirt and pulled it over my head, tossing it beside us as he pressed his chest against mine. I wasn't sure if it was his heart or mine that was hammering between us. His fingers slid between our bodies as he undid the button and zipper of my jeans. I did the same, undoing his pants with shaky fingers as we struggled to get closer to each other. I was terrified knowing what was about to happen, but I wanted it as much as he did.

He sat back on his knees as he tugged my jeans and panties down my hips. My arms covered my chest; I felt embarrassed about being so exposed to him. He smiled as he dragged my jeans down my legs then laid them on the grass beside us. His fingers looped around my wrists as he slowly pulled my arms away. "You're so beautiful," he said with sigh.

"Brock? Do you…do you have something?"

He laughed as he pulled his wallet from his back pocket and grabbed a condom that was tucked inside. He put it between his teeth the tear it open. "This is going to hurt, Bird. But I promise I'll take it slow."

I nodded as he leaned his body over mine. Propped up on his forearm, he slid his jeans over his hips and unrolled the condom over his length. He positioned himself at my entrance, and his lips found mine. He kissed me slowly, taking his time until my body relaxed beneath him. He rocked forward, and I wrapped my arms around his back, holding his chest against mine. I tensed, and he pulled back, his kisses slowing as we repeated the process. This time he pushed in farther, slipping the tip inside me then stopping, letting me get used to the feeling.

"Are you OK?" he asked, his voice strained, as if it were painful for him to hold back.

"Yes," I panted, and he rocked his hips, sliding farther inside me. I groaned as my body stretched and adjusted to accommodate him.

"This'll hurt, but only for a few minutes, OK?"

I nodded as his lips found mine again, pressing impossibly hard. He pushed against me, and I tried to cry out, but his kisses swallowed my words. His hips stilled, giving me time to get used to him as his lips left mine, peppering kisses over my eyelids and the tip of my nose. "I love you, Lie. I love you so much."

My eyes slowly opened as the pad of his thumb ran over my eyebrow. "I love you too." I didn't need to think about it as the words fell from my lips.

Between hungry kisses, we mumbled the words over and over as we made love under the moonlight. Flowing water drowned out heavy breaths, and rustling leaves masked the sounds of secret pleasures.

We lay in each other's arms for an hour afterward as I confessed what my life had been like over the past few weeks. His fingertips trailed up and down my arm, and occasionally he pressed his lips to my temple and reassured me that everything would be OK.

I wanted to believe him, but knowing he'd be leaving in a few days, I was stuck to face this on my own, and I didn't know if I'd be strong enough.

"I was ready to give up today," I told him, "before you called. I can't deal with it anymore. I can't face three more months of school."

Brock's arm stiffened as he pulled me to his side. I placed my leg over his waist and my head on his chest, wishing tonight would never end.

"I promised you I'd take care of you. I mean what I say." I looked up at him, and his eyes met mine. "You believe me, Bird?"

I nodded and lowered my head. There was nothing Brock could do to make this better. "I should get home. My mom will flip if she finds out I left."

I sat up and grabbed my jeans and underwear then pulled them on quickly as I looked for my shirt. "Oh, no!" I spotted it on a rock in the middle of the creek, soaking wet. Brock laughed as he stood up and buckled his jeans.

"Take mine." He bent down, grabbed his anarchy shirt, and held it out for me. I pulled it on quickly, loving that it smelled just like him. His fingers entwined with mine, and we made our way through the trees to my bike.

"I'm afraid I won't see you again," I told him. Tears clouded my vision, and Brock's hand slid over the side of my neck as he pulled me into his arms.

Covered in a thin layer of sweat, I awoke to the smell of coffee. I pushed my hair from my face as I glanced to the table beside my bed. There was a coffee cup, filled to the brim, and toast with jelly. I grabbed my cell phone, but it had died overnight, and in my hurry to leave the apartment, I'd forgotten to grab my charger.

I threw back my covers and grabbed a piece of the toast, taking a bite as I went into my bathroom and turned on the shower. Between bites I stripped down before tossing the crust into the small brushed-nickel trash can beside the sink.

I showered until the water ran cold, trying desperately to wash away the memories of my past. I dressed quickly and made my way downstairs, where Greg sat in his recliner, iPad in hand.

"Thanks for the breakfast."

"Where you off to?" he asked, as my hand landed on the door handle.

"I have classes, remember?"

As I looked at him in the daylight, my heart sank at his deteriorating appearance. He wasn't good at taking care of himself, and I wished he had found someone to marry so I didn't have to worry so much.

"'That wasn't breakfast. I assumed you had a hangover. Let me cook you something."

I chewed on my lip as I thought about being late for class. I had a few minutes to spare, and by the looks of my uncle, he didn't have much time himself. Regret settled in the pit of my stomach for my not having spent more time with him. He worried about me constantly, and the pain of my past had me avoiding him.

"How about I make breakfast for you? You were kind enough to let me stay with you."

"We're family, Lie. You're always welcome here." He grunted as he pushed himself up from his seat then shuffled toward the kitchen. My mother and Greg were night and day for siblings. Time hadn't been kind to him, and I suspected most of that was due to his health problems. I followed him to the kitchen and gestured for him to sit at the large glass table.

"When's the last time you saw a doctor?" I asked, as I pulled open the fridge and searched for food.

"Those quacks don't know anything." He laughed but soon had to clear his throat, fighting off a cough. "It's just a cold."

I stood with a bowl of sliced fruit and looked over at him. "A cold? You've been sick for a year, and you look like death."

"Gee, thanks, Lie."

"You know what I mean." I placed the fruit on the counter and turned back to the fridge to grab some yogurt. "If I'd knew you were this sick, I would have come to stay with you sooner."

"No one knew. I don't need any of those assholes in my business."

I shook my head as I kicked the fridge closed with my foot. "I can't blame you there." I grabbed two bowls from the cupboard and mixed the fruit into the vanilla yogurt.

"You should have heard the way they reacted when I said you'd come to stay with me." He nodded as I slid a bowl in front of him and slipped a spoon into it. "They acted like I was crazy for having you stay with me. They said you were dead to them." He shook his head, and a painful expression marred his face.

"It's fine." I waved away his worry. "What they think doesn't bother me anymore. I have everyone I need here." I gave him a weak smile and took a seat across from him, ignoring the thoughts of Brock that forced their way into my brain. "Good job at changing the subject." I bumped my shoulder against

Greg's, and he rumbled with a low laugh as he took a bite of his food. "So…the doctors?"

"Lie," he groaned, and shook his head. His eyes began to water as he dipped his head. "There's nothing they can do. It's part of life. Some are shorter than others."

Suddenly all my problems paled in comparison to his revelation. "I can't lose you too. You're all I have left." My hand shook, causing the spoon to rattle off a rhythm against the bowl, close to that of my racing heart.

He smiled weakly as his hand wrapped around my fingers to still them. "You have friends, and even if I do leave this damn place, you'll still have me." He used his other hand to point to my chest. "I'm in there."

A single tear rolled down my cheek, and I quickly brushed it away.

"I wish I could have had you as my daughter. I know I don't get to talk to you much lately, what with your being busy and growing up, but I want you to know how proud I am of you, Delilah."

"Proud?" I sniffled.

"Of course. I know life hasn't been easy for you. I blame myself." He squeezed my hand.

"How could you blame yourself? You didn't know."

"That's not an excuse. I knew how you came about in this world. A child needs a father figure in her life—and a decent mother for that matter."

"She was just a kid." I shook my head to rid the image of Brock's gray eyes from my thoughts. "Sometimes the truth isn't always that cut and dry."

"I'm just glad I get to spend the little time I have left on this earth with you." He kissed my forehead with dry, cracked lips then released my hand and cleared his throat again. He picked up his spoon and took a bite. I watched him for a moment before picking up my spoon as well.

"I'm glad I'm here with you too, Uncle Greg. For what it's worth, you make a good father."

He smiled as he shoved another bite into his mouth, and we finished our meal in silence.

I cleared our dishes and washed them quickly, not caring if I ran a little late to class. Greg settled back into his recliner as another fit of coughs racked his body.

"You want me to stay home today? We could watch movies and gossip about movie stars."

"Would a good dad let you skip school?" he asked playfully, and I stuck out my bottom lip.

"Take the Beamer. Keys are in the garage," he wheezed out.

"Thanks." I smiled, thankful I wouldn't have to take a bus.

"Hey. Promise me you'll call Marie today. I know there's stuff you'd rather not talk to me about, but you need to have someone."

In that moment I wished I could share all the painful memories that plagued me, but our relationship was just starting to blossom, and I didn't want to taint it. Greg was overwhelmed when he had thought my worst problems were a mean mother and a boyfriend who had broken my heart.

"If you promise me you'll call a doctor." I gave him a stern look.

He sighed loudly but smiled. "I'll do it for you. Promise you'll call her?"

I nodded as I stepped into the morning sun. I just wanted to get back to my routine; classes would be a great distraction. I typed the security code for the garage and pulled open the door.

There were three cars inside, and I smiled as my eyes landed on the silver Beamer. I'd always loved this car, but Greg always had been afraid to let me drive it.

I grabbed the keys and slid into the driver's seat. I hit the button next to the visor, and the large bay doors slid open. I backed out carefully and pressed the button again as I pulled out onto Sunnyside Road. It was a beautiful day, the clouds blocking the sun to keep it from being overbearingly hot. It probably wouldn't be long before they let loose.

I made it to campus as large drops began to patter against the windshield. I grabbed my purse and dug out a hair tie to throw my hair into a messy bun. I pulled down the visor and stared into the mirror as I gathered my hair and secured it at the back of my head. As I flipped the visor closed, I suddenly was staring into the eyes of a soaked Abel, his hands shoved into his jeans pockets. I froze, not sure what I should do next. My eyes fell to the keys that dangled from the ignition. I could run, like I always did. I glanced up again. The rain was coming down hard and heavy, but Abel stood still.

"Shit." I grabbed the keys and shoved them into my purse as I pushed the door open and made my way to the front of the car. "What are you doing here?"

"I go to school here, remember?"

"What do you want, Abel?"

"I'm sorry. I shouldn't have said any of those things to you last night."

"Little too late for that. Do you have any idea how scared I was of you with that gun? You have no idea. No idea." I shook my head as I tried to maintain my composure; I was dangerously close to losing it. I went to step around him, but he grabbed my arm and turned me toward him. His short-sleeve white shirt clung to his chest.

"Will you just stop for one fucking minute and listen to me? I fucked up, Lie. I know that. Let me try to make it right. Can we go somewhere dry and talk?"

"No. I'm done listening to your bullshit. I've had enough of you and Trish and all you other assholes."

He clenched his jaw as he smoothed back his wet hair. "You didn't have to run away, Lie. I won't go back to your place if that's what you want. I already told Trish we're done. You don't have to ever see me again, but please give me a chance to explain."

I pulled my arm from his grip. "I don't care who you fuck, Abel. Don't flatter yourself. I meant every word I just said. I don't care about you—either of you." I stormed off toward Gibson Hall and made it to my psych class just as the lecture was beginning. I slipped into a seat in the back near the door and dropped my purse onto the floor.

The door opened, and Abel looked around before his eyes landed on me and narrowed. He slipped into the desk beside me, and I adjusted in my seat to angle away from him.

"You aren't even in this class," I whispered angrily.

"Clearly I am. I'm sitting right here, Kettle."

"You're fucking hilarious." I rolled my eyes, and the guy in front of me turned around and narrowed his. I sneered and Abel laughed.

"I'm calling a truce."

"I'm not interested in being friends with a gun-toting drug dealer." I reached down to dig a pen from my bag along with a notepad. I'd left my book in the car, not thinking to grab it after I saw Abel. I flipped open the pad and poised my pen, ready to take notes.

"Come on, Lie," Abel whispered. "I'm trying to be the nice guy here. I'm trying."

"Don't strain yourself."

He smiled his panty-melting grin, and I wanted to smack him and my heart for fluttering.

"Fine. If I can't kill you with kindness, I'll take a different approach." He cleared his throat, and I shook my head. "Hey, there, Delilah," he began to sing, and my jaw dropped in horror as a few people turned around and looked at us.

"Stop it."

"Oh…it's what you do to me…"

"Damn it, Abel. Stop." I sank in my seat and covered my face with my hands to hide myself from prying eyes. I had no idea why he wouldn't want to follow in his mother's footsteps, because clearly he had inherited her talents.

Someone a few rows up knocked a book from his desk, and I jumped in my seat, my heart seizing in my chest. The flashbacks from the day that changed it all ran through my mind on an endless loop. I couldn't breathe, couldn't speak. Abel's fingers grabbed my arm.

"Lie, what's wrong? Lie? Was my singing that bad?"

I turned to him with tears in my eyes as I gasped for my next breath. I watched his expression transform from one of playfulness to panic.

"Hey, hey…I'm right here. It's OK. Come on. I'm going to take you out of here." Abel grabbed my bag and pulled me to my feet. I followed blindly behind him as we stepped outside. I sucked in a long breath and put my hands on my knees as I tried to block out the tragic memories that assaulted me.

"What's wrong, Lie? Tell me. What the hell was that?"

I shook my head and shoved him back from me as I squeezed my eyes closed. The rain had stopped, and the heat from the sun was starting to make me feel nauseous.

"Come on." Abel grasped my shoulders and began to walk me across the parking lot toward his car. I didn't fight him, because the last thing I wanted was to face anyone from my psych class. I'm sure they all thought I was a freak. So much for becoming someone new. We got into Abel's car, and still in a daze, I pulled on my seatbelt.

"You gonna tell me what happened back there?"

I shook my head as I stared out the passenger window. He sighed and started the engine then pulled out toward the road. I glanced at the glove compartment, and he reached across the seat and flipped it open.

"The gun is gone. If I had any idea how much it scared you, I would have tossed it the first day you found it." He drove for only a few minutes before pulling in at a hot dog stand that was a student favorite around here. "Look, I can't help you if you won't tell me what's going on."

"I don't need your help."

"If you say so."

"Whatever." I got out of the car, slamming the door behind me. Abel was soon at my side. "Why are we here?" I folded my arms over my chest.

"Hot dogs. Why else would we come to a hot dog stand?" he joked, and walked up to the window to order.

I sat at a picnic table as I waited for Abel to return with our food. If there were ever a time to run, my gut was telling me to run far and fast from him. But instead I waited for him to slide into the seat across from me. I tapped my fingers against the wooden top as a man at a nearby table took a bite of his food. I smiled down at his rat terrier, which was tied to a leash wrapped around his arm. The dog bared his teeth and let out a low, angry growl. His owner sat oblivious as he stuffed his face.

"Making friends?" Abel slid into the seat across from me with a grin.

"Why do people bring their pets out in public when they clearly shouldn't be around other people?" I snapped loudly, but the man ignored me.

"You're barking louder than the dog." Abel chuckled and snapped his fingers, causing the dog to lie down on the concrete.

"How did you do that?"

"Bitches love me." Abel winked as he slid my food over to me.

He picked up a hot dog and took a bite. "My mom never let me eat these when I was a kid."

I took a small bite, wishing I hadn't gotten out of bed this morning.

"She cared about you. You were lucky," I mumbled.

"Yeah, I was, but I didn't know it at the time. I just thought she was trying to stop me from having fun, ya know? It wasn't until I moved here that I realized how lucky I'd been, but it was too late."

"Is there a point you're trying to make?" I glanced up at him, and he smiled. A raindrop hit my cheek, and then rain began to pour down over us, soaking our food.

"You coming?" Abel pushed himself up from his seat but stopped when I didn't move.

"I like the rain."

"You're gonna catch a cold." He smirked, revealing one of his delicious dimples, his messy blond hair wet and hanging over his forehead.

"You don't get sick from the rain. That's an old wives' tale." I rolled my eyes and stayed put. I didn't know what I was trying to prove, but damn it, I was going to prove it.

Abel sighed dramatically as he took his seat across from me at the old picnic table.

"What are you doing?" I asked him.

"If you're not going, neither am I."

"Aren't you worried about getting sick?" I narrowed my eyes as I tried not to give into his playful mood.

"No, Lie. I'm worried about *you*." I rolled my eyes, and he laughed, shaking his head. "The *point,* Kettle, is that you have people who care about you and want to help you, but you're too damn stubborn to see it."

"Who? Like Trish?" I brushed some raindrops from my forehead.

"Like *me,* Lie. Me. If you'd open your goddamn eyes."

I looked up, his gaze intense as he stared back at me. "I don't want you to rescue me, Abel. I just want to be left the hell alone."

"Why? Because you have Brock? Some asshole who won't even come see you?"

"He can't."

"Why? Why can't he, Lie? Because if you were mine, I couldn't go a fucking day without being able to see you."

I pushed from my seat, completely drenched and boiling with anger. "Yeah, well, Brock can't visit me because he's in prison. You happy now? There's the pathetic fucking truth. I'm alone. I've been alone this whole damn time, and your little stunt with that gun brought everything back." I fisted my hands in my hair, gripping tightly as I gritted my teeth. "Goddamn it, Abel. You're the exact opposite of what I need."

He stood as my hands covered my face to hide the tears. He was by my side, his fingers wrapping around my wrist.

"Don't hide yourself from me, Lie." He tugged on my hand, and I let it fall.

"It's not that simple," I told him.

"It is. It is that simple. You choose to keep me out." He wrapped his arms around me and pulled me against his chest. "Jesus Christ, Lie. I'm so sorry."

I shook my head but couldn't bring myself to pull out of his grasp.

"You may not want anyone to care," he said, "but it's too late for that. Let me take you home. You don't have to tell me anything, but I have so much I want to say."

"You scared me," I whispered against his chest, and his grip on me tightened as his other hand went to my hair, stroking it softly.

"I know, Kettle." I felt his lips press against the top of my head. "I'm so sorry."

Chapter Fourteen

Screaming Fears

We drove to Abel's house in silence. I was swimming with anger, sadness, and regrets of the past—stuck in limbo. Everyone sees life through his or her own experiences. Some grow and learn to live in the moment, like Abel. He knew how precious every second was and didn't stop to think about tomorrow. I stayed fixed in the past, forever haunted by the things that had brought me down.

I knew if I could just open up and let him in, we could balance each other. But that was easier said than done. Knowing what needed to be done and doing it were separated by fear— fear of the past, the unknown. I was too angry, too stubborn to give him the chance.

I glanced around the living room. New sheets of plywood leaned against a wall, covering an old fireplace. New molding had been added around the ceiling.

"It takes time," Abel said, "but I'm getting there."

"I'd sell it and buy something new."

"Yeah." He glanced around as he rubbed his hand over his jaw. "You probably would. You're good at running."

"You don't know anything about me," I snapped.

"I deserve that." Abel cringed, and I hated myself for taking a jab at him. Old habits die hard.

"No, you didn't." I sighed. "It's hard to let the walls down."

"You're in luck." Abel walked through the living room to a smaller room that sat behind it. I followed, stopping in the doorway as he picked up a sledgehammer that had a handle at least three feet long. "I happen to be a semiprofessional wall remover, Kettle. It's a very prestigious title, not to be taken lightly." He smirked, the dimples in his cheeks settling in deeply.

"Really? You brought me here to work?" I crossed my arms over my chest. "You gonna force me at gunpoint?" I quipped.

"You'll feel better, I promise." He shook his head, as he tried not to laugh at my anger.

I rolled my eyes and took a step toward him, holding out my hand for the hammer. I took it from his grip, and it immediately hit the floor.

"Jeez, it's heavier than I expected."

Abel winked as his tongue ran over his lips. "I don't get many complaints."

"Whatever." I gripped the sledgehammer with both hands but could barely lift it from the floor.

"OK. Don't hurt yourself, Kettle. Let's start with something smaller." He leaned the large hammer against the wall and handed me a smaller version.

"This is better." I smiled as Abel picked up the larger sledgehammer and held it in two hands.

"We're gonna take down this little wall here to open it up into what will be the formal dining room. With each swing you say something that scares you or has hurt you. Got it? I'll go first."

I nodded, my teeth digging into my lower lip as Abel stepped toward the wall. "It wasn't fair that my entire life was taken from me." He swung hard, the sledgehammer digging into the drywall and causing it to crumble around the head of the hammer. He stepped back, panting. "Your turn."

I stepped forward, the hammer in my hands as I looked at the huge hole Abel had left. "I hate...that..." I sighed and held the hammer at my side. I swung it up to my shoulder and adjusted my footing. "I hate that you won't just go away." I swung, the hammer stopping abruptly as it lodged into the wall next to Abel's crater. I tugged on it twice before it came loose and swung down to my side.

"Fair enough." He stepped forward, and I pressed myself against the side wall. He rolled his head from shoulder to shoulder, stretching his neck. "This one is for my grandpa thinking I was too spoiled and needed to learn to live like him." He swung and hit just a few inches from his first mark. "Would've been nice not to have to deal drugs to survive just because he hated my dad." He pulled up his damp, white shirt and wiped it over his brow. I tried not to stare at his abs as he walked by me and grabbed a gallon of water from the mantel and guzzled a large swig.

I positioned myself in front of the wall. "This is for my mom. It wasn't my fault she was raped. I still deserved to be loved." I swung hard, throwing all my anger into my swing. The hammer wedged into Abel's growing crater. He walked up beside me with the water in his hand. I took it and drank a sip.

"That was better." He motioned for me to move back, and I stepped back to the side wall as I waited for him to swing. He focused on the wall as his eyebrows pulled together.

"This is for scaring you last night, Kettle." He swung, and the sound of the hammer hitting the wall echoed in my heartbeat. He observed the hole in the wall as he stepped back. He propped the hammer next to me as he pulled his shirt over his head and tossed it on top of an old paint bucket.

"This is for everyone who bullied me in school." I stepped forward and took a swing, surprised at how much my muscles burned and how the pressure from my chest was beginning to ease. I glanced over my shoulder at Abel, whose body glistened with a fresh layer of sweat, his jeans hanging low on his hips.

"This…" He glanced down at the hammer and back at me as he took his position in front of the wall. "This is for not being able to save them."

My heart sank as he swung, the hammer breaking through to the next room. I hadn't realized how much he'd been holding back.

Our eyes locked, and I nodded as a tear stung my eye. "This is also for not being able to save them." I broke eye contact and took my shot, but my arms were growing weaker, and I barely made a dent. My eyes met Abel's again, and he looked confused but quickly masked his reaction.

"That all you got, slugger?" Abel winked as he switched positions with me. "This is for…Becca." He swung, knocking a basketball-size hole in the wall. Panting with exhaustion, he dropped the sledgehammer at his side.

"You brought up Becca to James. Who was she?" I asked, as I tucked my damp hair behind my ear.

"That's not how this game works, Kettle." He scratched the back of his head as he released a frustrated sigh. "Becca was my girlfriend. She's the reason I gave up selling. What I had that night I met you...and what was in the car—that was the last of it. I was telling you the truth."

"She didn't approve?"

"It's not exactly an honorable profession. I'd finally gotten my inheritance, and there was no reason anymore. Becca was on my case about stopping." He nodded, and his hand ran over his jaw. "She trusted me." He picked up the hammer and swung at the wall, connecting with a grunt. "She shouldn't have."

I stared at him as his eyes dropped to the floor. "You're not a bad guy, Abel."

"Not a good guy either, Lie."

"You...want to talk about it?" I grabbed the jug of water and held it out for him. He nodded a thanks and took a drink.

"Not much to say. Boy meets girl. Boy lies and loses the only person who gave a damn about him." He smiled sadly. "One night we went to bed, and while I slept, she went through my phone. The next morning I woke up alone in bed." He tapped the head of the sledgehammer against the floor like he was debating whether to finish his story. "I found James and Becca practically fucking in the spare bedroom. She was fucked up out of her mind. She did it to get back at me." He shrugged, and I saw him fight back the sadness.

"Why would you blame yourself for that?" I took a step toward him, and his gaze met mine, stopping me.

"I promised her I'd go straight, and I lied. The fucked-up part was that I didn't need to do it anymore. I became addicted to being needed, ya know? I grew up in the in-crowd, and after being on the outside for many years, I didn't want to step away from it again. I lost it—I beat the hell out of James. Becca never talked to me again."

"Ouch."

"Yeah. It was a shitty night." He smirked, but I knew he was hurting. "You should choose your friends more wisely, Kettle."

I rolled my eyes as I stepped next to him and nudged him with my hip. "Who said we were friends?" I joked, as I looked over my shoulder to make sure he was out of the way.

"Funny girl."

I lifted my hammer to take aim at the wall. I was grateful Abel had opened up to me, but I wasn't sure I could do the same. "I think I'm too tired to do this again," I said.

"You want to take a shower? Get out of the wet clothes?"

"If that's some lame attempt to get me naked, it's not going to work."

"Suit yourself. I'm going to make something to eat. Bathroom is upstairs, and you're welcome to anything in my dresser." He propped his hammer against the wall and walked out of the room. I felt like a jerk for not sharing anything more with him, but I couldn't form the words.

I made my way upstairs and into his bedroom. I grabbed some clothes from his dresser, a large gray T-shirt and a pair of black boxer briefs. Under the clothes was a tattered picture, and I pulled it out to look at a young Abel with his parents. His mother was smiling, with her arm over his shoulder. His father stood on the other side of her, his arm around her waist. I heard a noise from downstairs and slid the picture back where I'd found it and tiptoed from the room and into the bathroom.

I stripped off my damp clothes and put them in a pile by the door. I made the shower as hot as possible and stepped under the water. I hated how easy it was for Abel to let me in, and I was unable to do the same. I knew it pained him to talk about his past, but he was willing to do it just to make me feel better. I washed away the memories of my past and quickly dressed.

As I slipped down the steps, I caught sight of Abel, his shirtless back to me in the kitchen.

"What ya making?" I asked, as he spun around and shot me a lopsided grin.

"Well, it's no spaghetti, but raviolis are always a favorite." He held up a can, and I shook my head as I walked into the kitchen and sat at the island.

"You have horrible eating habits," I joked, as he slid a bowl in front of me.

"Yeah, well…that's a fact. I'm gonna take a quick shower. Hope you saved me some hot water." His hand fell on my shoulder as he walked around me, and I grimaced, knowing there was none left. A few minutes later, Abel came downstairs with my damp clothes. Then I heard a dryer begin to run before he disappeared up the steps again.

I pushed my food around the bowl, my stomach twisted in knots as I thought about finally telling someone about my past. Becoming someone new didn't make anything go away. It didn't change anything. I couldn't escape what had happened, and keeping it to myself made my life a miserable and lonely existence.

Abel came back down the steps a few minutes later, wearing nothing but a pair of hunter-green boxers, drops of water dotting his tanned skin. "Why aren't you eating?" he asked, as he pulled open the fridge and bent over, pushing around the contents inside. He stood, a soda in hand as he cracked open the can and took a drink.

"Do you think things happen for a reason?" I asked, glancing up at him and back to my bowl.

"No. Not at all." The muscles in his jaw jumped under his skin.

"You don't think this is all part of some big plan?"

Abel laughed sardonically as he shook his head and took another drink. "What plan, Kettle? What plan is there that involves destroying a family? What plan would ever involve hurting you?"

I shrugged as I took a bite of my food. "The hardest part is that I still care about him." I chanced a glance at him, and he looked deep in thought. "It wasn't me he hurt, Abel." His gaze snapped to mine.

"I'd have to disagree with you on that."

"I don't even know where to begin." I shook my head as a tear slipped from my eye and rolled down my cheek.

"How did you two meet?" he asked, as he sat on the stool across from me. I ate as I slowly recounted the events that had brought me to Brock. I expected sarcastic remarks, but Abel just listened as I told him how I'd run away and ended up in the shelter. It was embarrassing to say it out loud, but he knew about struggling.

I pushed my bowl aside, and Abel stood, taking my hand and pulling me to the front door. I sat next to him on the porch steps as he lit a cigarette and held it out to me. I shook my head as I folded my arms and rested them on my knees.

"It feels like life ended when things went sideways."

He took a drag, surrounding us in a cloud of smoke. "It feels like mine is finally beginning," he said quietly.

"Must be nice." I thought of Abel and Trish together, and the idea of it turned my stomach, but I still refused to admit to myself why. He deserved to be happy. As frustrating as he was, he really was a good person; he just couldn't see it.

Shaking his head, he pulled another drag from his cigarette and ran his free hand over his damp hair.

"What?" I studied his profile.

"It's not easy, Lie. None of this is fucking easy, but I'm trying."

"So am I."

He pushed to his feet as he flicked his cigarette into the grass and turned to go back inside. "Bullshit." The door closed behind him, and I felt like all the air had been pushed from my lungs.

All my confusion became clouded by anger because that was easier than facing the truth. The truth was that he was right. I opened the door and went inside, determined to tell him to go fuck himself once and for all. Abel stood just inside, his back to me with his hands in his hair.

"What the fuck is your problem?" I spat, and he turned around, his eyes glazed over with unshed tears.

"You. You're my fucking problem, Lie." His tone softened. "*You*." He took a step toward me, his large, warm hands sliding over my cheeks as his lips pressed hard and desperately against mine. My knees threatened to give out as my lips moved against his on their own accord.

It took only a few seconds for me to come to my senses, and I pushed against his chest, angry, but not exactly sure why.

"What do you think you're doing?" I shouted, as I shoved back harder.

"What I've been wanting to do since the moment I met you."

"Funny, because you had the opportunity to kiss me the night we met, and instead you made a fool out of me in front of my only friend."

Abel's expression turned angry as he pointed at my chest, and I pushed my back against the door. "I'm your friend, Lie. *I'm* your friend, but you're too damn stubborn to let me in."

"The last time I let someone in, a lot of people got hurt," I shouted back with just as much anger.

"I'm not Brock, Delilah. I'm not him!" His voice echoed off the walls in the nearly empty house.

"You're not. So stop trying to be, and leave me the hell alone!" Anger flowed through my veins, but I knew it wasn't him I was mad at. I was mad at myself, because try as I might, I had feelings for this guy.

"You don't mean that."

"I do, Abel. I mean it."

He closed the gap between us as he swallowed hard. "You think if you keep saying it, I'll suddenly stop caring? It doesn't work that way, Kettle. Trust me—I'm fucking torturing myself here, and I can't stop. I'm falling for you. If it were that easy, I would have walked away by now."

His last sentence cut deep, but I deserved it. He was hurting from his own past, and I wasn't helping him. "Abel…" My voice shook as I stared into his stormy ocean-colored eyes. "What happened to you wasn't your fault. But me…" My voice trailed off as I squeezed my eyes shut and forced myself to continue. My eyes slowly opened as his feather-soft fingers slid over my jaw. "I'm responsible for what happened."

"You can't believe that. You can't control what other people do."

My hand covered his, intertwining our fingers and pulling his hand from my face. "I can prove you wrong." I smiled sadly as his eyebrows knitted. I stepped around him and grabbed my purse. With shaky fingers I called Marie.

"Can I see you?" My eyes met Abel's as he leaned against the archway to the living room. "I think I'm ready."

"I can be at the office in twenty minutes, Delilah."

I nodded, even though she couldn't see it. "I want to bring along someone…a friend."

"All right."

"All right," I repeated then hung up and slid my phone into my purse.

"Where are we going?" Abel asked as he pushed himself from the wall. I walked around him to where I'd heard the dryer running earlier and grabbed my clothes.

"We're going to go see Marie, my therapist, and I'm going to tell you what happened to me."

Abel nodded and went up the stairs to get dressed. I let my fake smile fall as I undressed and pulled on my own clothing. There was no doubt this would end whatever it was we had, and as much as I tried to convince myself that was what I wanted it, the stabbing pain in my chest disagreed.

Chapter Fifteen

Facing Demons

Abel didn't make chitchat as we drove across town to Marie's office. I stared out the passenger window of his old muscle car, wishing we could drive to a new town or state where no one knew us, but it was finally time to stop running.

When we arrived I unbuckled my seatbelt but didn't move. This was going to be excruciating, and even though Abel believed I wasn't a bad person, there was little doubt that he'd soon change his mind.

"I'm right here, Lie. I'm not going anywhere." He reached over and grabbed my hand.

"I know," I lied, because that's what I did. I gave him a weak smile and pushed open my door, letting my fingers slip from his grasp for what I knew was the last time.

I slowly made my way up the steps with Abel behind me, his hand on the small of my back. My lips still tingled from his kiss, and I wanted to turn around and press them back against his again, but I dragged myself to the door.

I stepped inside, and Abel pulled the door closed behind me.

"I'm in my office," Marie called out.

"Last chance to run away," I told Abel.

"Not a chance." He chuckled as we stepped inside her office.

"Marie, this is Abel. Abel, that's Marie." I watched as she stood to shake his hand.

"I'm ready." I didn't need to elaborate. I knew Marie had been waiting for me to finally talk about that day when everything had gone wrong. I never wanted to say the words out loud for fear of admitting Brock was no longer by my side. Guilt had eaten away at me every day for missing him.

"Take your time, Delilah," Marie said with a blank face, but I knew she was pleased. How could she not be? She had worked for months to get me to this point.

My hands shook as I sat down in the oversize black vinyl chair across the room. My eyes focused on a small fountain that was meant to be soothing, but every time I heard it, it made me need to go to the bathroom. Abel leaned against the large bay window, his eyes scanning the surroundings.

"Brock told me not to go to school that day." I cleared my throat and dared a glance at Marie. Her pen was poised in her hand, but she stared intently at me, not writing. "I had a huge fight with my mom the night before. She found out that I had snuck out to see him." I rolled my eyes as I peeled the light-pink nail polish from my thumbnail. "Anyway…" A lump formed in my throat, and I swallowed hard, trying to keep my tears at bay. "I couldn't stay home, not when she was so mad at me."

I pushed myself up from my seat and hurried over to the water cooler in the corner of the room. I filled a paper cup and chugged down the cool liquid before tossing the cup into the wastebasket. I stared out the window, my arms over my chest, my eyes unfocused. I felt Abel's eyes on me from the other end of the bay window, but I couldn't look at him. If I did, I knew I wouldn't be able to continue.

"I was late." Outside it had started to drizzle, and I watched as tiny drops smacked the glass and trickled together before sliding out of view. "Class had started. Ms. Campbell was really strict." I peeled the remaining flecks of polish from my nail, unsure if I could go on.

"Casey Campbell," Marie said. She wasn't asking me a question, but I nodded anyway. It was weird to hear her call a teacher by her first name.

"She was married," I said, glancing back at Marie, whose expression hadn't changed. "By the end of first period, I was dying to leave. I was worried that maybe Brock wanted to see me, and that was why he wanted me to stay home. I was afraid he'd hate me if he found out I went anyway."

"Why would he hate you?"

"Why did anyone hate me?" I shrugged and let out a humorless laugh. "They just did."

"Brock had proven himself to be different, hadn't he?" Marie asked.

I nodded as a tear slid down my cheek. Brock was different from anyone I'd known. "He treated me like I was the most important person in the world." I glanced at Abel's expressionless face and back at Marie.

"Perhaps to him you were."

"If I were, he wouldn't have done what he did. He wouldn't have left me."

"Do you blame him?"

"For leaving me? Of course I do!" I spun around and glared at her.

"No. Do you blame him for what happened, or do you still blame yourself?"

"I don't know anymore," I said.

Marie smiled, looking pleased with my answer.

"You're the only person who doesn't judge him—or me for that matter." I glanced at my shaky fingers as I balled my hands into fists, trying to stop them from revealing how scared I was.

"It isn't my job to judge," she said. "We all do things in life that we regret. We all make mistakes. That's what makes us human."

"Most would argue that Brock wasn't."

"That he wasn't regretful?"

"That he wasn't human."

Marie shrugged. "Well, it's easy to vilify people, to place blame. That's human nature as well."

"They blamed me." Another warm tear slid down my cheek, and I resisted the urge to wipe it away. I was so tired of hiding my pain.

"You can't control how others feel about you. What's important is how you feel about yourself." She adjusted in her seat, and I felt her eyes burn into me. "He didn't leave you, Delilah."

I sighed as I picked up a small brass cat that sat on the windowsill. My mother collected pointless little things like this. I suddenly had the urge to throw it against the window. My fingers curled around the knickknack as my knuckles turned white.

"Delilah, are you hearing me?"

"It's 'Lie.' Everyone calls me 'Lie.'" My voice was quiet and sad. It sounded strange hearing how weak I'd become over Brock.

"That's a rather sad name for someone, don't you think?"

"Not if it's the truth." I put the brass cat back in its place and ran my fingertips down the curve of its back.

"If it's the truth, how can it be a lie?"

"You're not making any sense, Marie. Maybe you need someone to talk to."

My words dripped with sarcasm, and I smiled. Something about Marie made me feel safe. She never judged; she only asked questions to help me understand myself better. She was comforting, like a favorite blanket to hide under when you're scared of the dark. Brock had been that for me, and now Marie had stepped into that role. But she was teaching me to learn to face the fears and stand on my own. Brock only wanted to shelter me from the real world and keep me from ever facing my demons.

"I'll keep that in mind, Delilah." She cocked an eyebrow as she leaned forward to retrieve her glass of water from the small table in front of her. It struck me as odd, and my eyes focused on the intricate glass with rose etchings.

"Beautiful, isn't it?" she asked, and I only nodded. Marie and I weren't friends. There was a reason she sat with a table between us, her drinking from a fancy glass and me from a paper cup. Perhaps she was worried I'd break it and use it as a weapon. I'd bet money that when I came in next week, the brass cat would be gone. I shook the thought from my head.

"Tell me about lunch." Marie sat back in her seat, crossing one leg over the other.

"It's the second meal of the day."

"Delilah…" Her voice was stern but soft. She sounded like one of those TV moms—the ones who hug their kids when they're sad and ground them from their favorite toy when they break some obscure rule.

"The cafeteria was nearly empty when I got to lunch." My voice cracked, and I hated how weak I sounded. "I can still smell the sloppy joes we had that day. I remember being excited because my mom never made those at home. She barely knew how to cook anything, so we always had mac and cheese or hot dogs." I smiled sardonically as I looked down at my Chuck Taylors. My new pair, which I wore today, were blue. The ones I'd worn in high school were white.

"When you grow up where I did, you learn to appreciate the little things. Anyway…" I shook my head. I'd gotten sidetracked. I glanced at Abel. His eyes were fixed on me, and only concern marred his beautiful face. "Shelly sought me out again. It was like a favorite hobby of hers to torture me." I rolled my eyes, but I couldn't hide the pain I felt at the memory. I took my seat as I prepared to relive that painful day.

"I see you haven't killed yourself yet. Pity,'" she said with a glare. I swallowed against the lump in my throat.

"Please don't. Not today, Shelly," I begged, hoping for once that she could see the pain I was in. Fighting with my mom and now knowing I would lose Brock in only a few days—I couldn't handle any more than that.

"Oh, how cute. You think I care." Her lips formed an evil smirk. I jumped, as it sounded like one of the cafeteria doors slammed closed, but Shelly just looked at me, sadness and confusion replacing her wicked grin.

"Shelly?" I said, and her hand went to the table. As my eyes fell, I saw her pink fitted Polo shirt begin to turn red around her shoulder. "Shelly?" I said with more panic as the loud slamming sound grew. The next thing I knew, it was chaos. The sounds of screaming

filled the air, punctuated by the ear-piercing bangs that rumbled like thunder through the cavernous space.

I slid under the bench seat of the table, and my eyes locked with Shelly's. She looked oddly peaceful, in shock maybe. I reached for her hand and helped her crawl under the table beside me as my hand went to her damp, crimson shoulder.

"What's happening?" she asked, her voice shaking.

"I don't know."

"It hurts."

Tears rolled down her cheeks, and I pulled her in for a hug. It was a strange feeling, hugging the girl who, just the day before, had made me contemplate killing myself. Her fingers dug painfully into my sides as my thoughts raced.

Bang.

Screams.

Bang.

Someone fell beside the table, and I recognized the lifeless eyes of Danny London, his eyes fixed on mine, unmoving.

Whoever was shooting was yelling over the noise, but I couldn't make out what they were saying until a pair of old, worn black boots stepped next to Danny's body. They kicked at his side, and he didn't move. I struggled to hold my breath as Shelly cried cry hysterically. I put my hand over her mouth just as the gunman sunk to his knees and bent his head down.

I stared into Brock's stormy gray eyes as confusion and anger flashed across his face.

"Bird, you weren't supposed to be here." His voice was eerily calm, like the way he used to talk to me in the shelter when I'd been upset.

I squeezed Shelly tighter as my heart seized in my chest. The pain was excruciating. I opened my mouth, trying to find words, *but Brock placed his finger over his lips to tell me to be quiet as he winked and stood up.*

More shots rang out, and I tasted bile as it rose in my throat. I pried Shelly's fingers from my skin. Her face was gray, and her breathing was shallow.

"Be very quiet," I said, as I brushed her blood-sticky hair from her face. "I have to…" A sob ripped through my chest. "I have to go help." My words were garbled from the next sob as I struggled not to completely lose my mind.

Two minutes ago I hated this girl, and for reasons unknown, she hated me. Now I was trying to comfort her. I gripped the bench seat with shaky hands as I pulled myself up between it and the table. Crowds of people blocked the doorway as they struggled to flee the cafeteria. That just made them a bigger target. I screamed, but I couldn't even hear my own voice. The smell of cafeteria food and the blood that was smeared across my body was turning my stomach, and I had to stop myself from retching. Someone had bumped against one of the light switches, and half the room was now dark.

"Brock…" My voice broke, and the wind was knocked from my lungs as I was pushed to the floor. A boy I didn't know gave me an apologetic look as he stepped on my hand and ran for the doorway.

Tears streamed down my face, as I tripped on the cold tile floor and gripped my stomach.

My arms wrapped tightly around my stomach as I rocked in my chair, oblivious to how insane I must have looked.

"You tried to help them," Marie's voice broke the silence, and my teary eyes met hers as I nodded slowly.

"I had to try. It was my fault."

Marie shook her head, and Abel took a step toward me, but Marie cut her gaze to him, and he stopped. "Brock was troubled, Delilah. You didn't cause his problems, and you couldn't stop him. No one could have after he made the decision to do what he did."

"That's not true. He did it because they bullied me."

"So you think they deserved what happened?"

I shoved myself up from my seat, enraged. "Of course they didn't!"

"Exactly my point," she replied calmly. "You wouldn't have wished that on them. You aren't to blame. Not for what happened to them and not for what happened to you."

I fell back into my seat, but the aching in my stomach only grew more painful as I struggled for a breath that wouldn't come.

"Let me get you some water." Abel fumbled with the paper cups at the water cooler, but Marie held up her hand.

"She'll be fine." Her voice was assertive, unlike I'd ever heard her before. Abel froze, cup in hand.

I doubled over as my gasping grew louder, and tiny crimson drops fell on the knees of my jeans. I looked up to Marie for help, but she sat unmoving. My trembling fingers ran over my lower lip, and I pulled them back to examine the smattering of blood.

"I'm bleeding. Why am I bleeding?" My voice was shrill with terror, but Marie and Abel seemed unconcerned.

"You're doing great, Delilah. Tell me what happened next."

I shook my head as my body trembled like a leaf in a hurricane. I squeezed my eyes closed and tried again to fill my lungs. When my chest expanded, the sound that left my throat was that of a crying child, and I was able to once again speak.

I reached my injured hand out to my left, toward where Shelly hid, the bright overhead lighting causing me to squint. Her head was propped unnaturally against the bench, and her eyes were half open and fixed on nothingness, her skin ash gray.

The bright light slowly faded, as if we were in an eclipse, as Brock knelt over me, his tears dripping onto my face and running over the bridge of my nose.

"Bird! Bird, I'm so sorry." He pulled me roughly into his chest as I gasped for air. His body shook, and I closed my eyes, lulled to sleep with the thudding rhythm of his hammering heart. "I love you so much, Bird." A sob cut through his words. I tried to open my heavy eyes, so I could tell him it would be OK. It didn't even hurt anymore. But I was unable to form any words as his arm rose, quivering as he pressed the handgun to his temple. "I'm so sorry." His finger pressed the trigger, his eyes locked on mine.

Bang.

My body fell to back to the hard tile, sprawled over Brock's legs in a twisted heap of broken hearts and unkeepable promises. The steady beating of his love faded into silence along with our future.

I glanced at my trembling hand, which still clutched my stomach, the blood gone from my fingers. The small crimson circles that had spattered on my jeans had vanished. I took in an easy breath as I looked up at Marie.

"It wasn't your fault, Delilah. You couldn't save them. You couldn't save yourself."

A chill ran through me, and it felt like the temperature had dropped at least ten degrees as realization settled in.

A warm, strong hand wrapped around mine as Abel sank to his knees next to me. He brushed my hair from my face and tucked it behind my ear. It was then I realized the dark-chocolate curtain that had blocked him from view. I looked over at him through uncertain eyes, and he smiled that heart-melting smile.

"You don't need to hide anymore," he said.

I pushed myself to my feet and studied my face in the mirror that hung above Marie's filing cabinet. Sure enough, my hair was as dark as the day I was born, hanging perfectly straight and framing my sad face. Abel stepped behind me, his head over mine, and it reminded me of the day we'd brushed our teeth at the apartment. Trish…Abel…I spun around and looked up at him, unable to ask the question that hung like thick humidity between us. He smiled sadly as he ran his knuckles softly over my cheek.

"You? The boat…" My eyes searched his as he shook his head and looked at the floor between us.

"I know I have boyish good looks, but I don't look thirteen, do I?" he joked, but his smile fell. "No. That night Becca cheated on me, I couldn't cope. I lost it when I confronted James, and it cost me my life."

"The gun," I whispered, as my eyes searched his. "Did you…"

"No. James did. He shot me point blank." His hand ran over the back of his head.

"But he's…Is he like us?"

"Yeah. He hanged himself a week later."

My hand flew over my mouth as I inhaled a sharp breath. "Brock…"

Abel pulled me into his chest, wrapping his arms around me.

Marie placed her hand on my back. "You did well, Delilah."

I clung to Abel as he pulled me from the office and into the blinding sun. We didn't speak during the entire trip back to his home.

We pulled up outside of Abel's old fixer-upper, and for the first time, I truly saw why this place was so important to him. Being damaged and broken doesn't mean something is worthless.

I got out and stretched in the warm summer sun. Abel was by my side and laced his fingers in mine.

"What happens now?" My voice shook as I tried to process everything we'd been through.

He smiled down at me, the dimples that made me swoon settling in his cheeks. "Now you get your happily ever after." He winked, and my stomach fluttered.

"But where? I mean…do I have to go back to Mississippi?"

Abel sighed as his eyes roamed over the house. "I'm not in California, am I? I like it here. This is my happy place now." He glanced down at me and back at the building as he squeezed my hand.

"Where would I stay? What about Trish and my uncle?"

"You stay where you have the happiest memories and help others like I do, Kettle. Trish still has a chance if she makes a few changes in her life, but your uncle has been hanging on only for you. You need to let him go."

"How can I just let someone go, Abel? How can I let him die?"

"Not everyone has a choice. Sometimes bad things happen. It's not like he'll be gone forever." He smiled down at me.

"You and I are both…"

"It's a lot to take in right now. You have all the time in the world to ask questions. Don't you want to take a day off? Rest? It's Sunday," he quipped.

"Very clever."

I thought that over as looked down at my tattered blue shoes. My thoughts went briefly to Brock, but try as I might, I knew all my memories were convoluted, and I had projected a savior image onto someone who needed saving himself. Abel's thumb softly slid over the back of my hand, and I took a tentative step forward. My smile grew as I took another, pulling him behind me. I practically could smell the fresh paint that would go on the walls, see the lilies that would bloom in the flower bed near the porch.

Abel pulled open the door and waited for me to slip inside. I stopped at the base of the stairs and turned to him. "What about Trish?" I asked in a panic.

He took a step forward and sighed as his hands fell on my hips.

"Are we all? I mean, is everyone...?"

"No." He laughed. "This is the same old sunny Florida. Some are like us—like James. Others are just...on the edge. Those are the ones, like Trish, that we can interact with. We can help push them in the right direction or be here to welcome them when the inevitable happens."

"So is this like...heaven or something?"

"Hardly. The weather here kind of sucks." He laughed, and I pushed against his chest.

"I'm glad you think all of this is so funny."

"I've had time to get used to it. You will too. Give it time."

My eyes glanced around the old house as I felt a fresh wave of sadness wash over me like Abel's ocean eyes were doing right now. "Do you mind if I stay here with you for a while?"

He tucked my hair behind my ears as he lowered his face, his lips pressing gently against mine. It felt like being kissed for the first time all over again. My heart raced in my chest as my head swam with euphoria.

I slipped my hands up Abel's chest and behind his neck as I pulled him closer. He was wrong about one thing. This moment, with my lips against his, was heaven.

Epilogue

I felt the change in the air as I stepped out of the car in Mississippi. The weight I'd carried around with me was gone, but sadness filled that void. I needed to see Brock, and I needed to get closure for what we'd been through if I wanted to move on.

Abel's long fingers wrapped around mine, and he squeezed them gently. I glanced up at him, and he smiled as his free hand brushed the brown locks from my face.

"Are you sure you want to do this?" he asked, as his green-blue eyes danced over mine. I loved staring into them. They were deep like the ocean and full of the unknown but always calm.

"I'm sure." I nodded as my hand rested on his chest. "I want to be able to move forward with you."

His jaw clenched, and the muscles ticked under his skin. He didn't want me to see Brock, but he wanted to be with me just as much as I wanted him. This was the only way. His hands came up to hold my face as he studied my eyes.

"I love you, Lie."

"I love you too, Abel." I placed my hand over one of his as I smiled up at him. "I'll be OK." He nodded as his hands fell to his sides; then he shoved them into his pockets.

I stared at the massive gray building that stood before me, the color matching Brock's eyes.

I pulled open the heavy door, and my eyes landed on a woman behind a thick glass window. She glanced up toward me but seemed unconcerned and went back to typing on her computer. I swallowed hard as I approached her, the walls feeling like they were closing in on me.

"I'm here to see Brock Ryan." My voice cracked as I spoke, and I hated myself for letting her see how nervous I was.

Her fingers clicked away on the keys as she searched her records for his name. My eyes danced over the man who stood a few feet away from me, a gun holstered on his hip. He glanced at me and down at his weapon when he saw me staring.

"Guns make me nervous." I looked back at the heavyset woman.

"They can't hurt you now, sweetie. Go through those doors. Someone will direct you where to go from there."

"Thank you." I pushed my purse higher on my shoulder as I turned to the next set of doorways.

I was in a daze as I was being searched and sent off through another set of doors. The room was long and narrow, a glass wall dividing one side from the other.

"Seat three," the woman behind me called out, and I nodded as I made my way to the third little desk with a phone on the wall. There were others in the room waiting to visit their loved ones, and I clutched my hands against my stomach as my nerves began to get the better of me, or maybe it was the memory of the shot that ended my life.

"I can't wait until we get out of here." I sighed as I looked around the shelter.

"I like that... 'we.'" Brock smiled at me, and a girlish giggle escaped my lips. *"You're driving me crazy, Bird."* His fingertip slid over the tip of my nose playfully. *"It's like you're in my veins. I don't know what I'd do without you."*

The door on the other side of the glass opened, and a row of men filed in, taking their seats across from their visitors. My heart stopped in my chest as my eyes locked on his beautiful, sad, gray eyes. He smiled, but it didn't reach his eyes, and sat down across from me. With the glass it was like he was a million miles away, but I was transported back to that last night I'd spent with him. It felt like we were still together, clinging to hope of a future that never would come to pass.

His cold stare was fixed on me as I slowly picked up the phone on the wall beside me. After a second he did the same and slowly raised it to his ear.

"You look...the same." I don't know why I said it. Time meant nothing to us now.

"You look different. You're...happy," was all he said as his gaze fell to my lips.

"I am."

"You aren't supposed to be here, Bird." He glanced around before leaning on his elbows.

"Why did you do it?" I asked, my voice getting caught in my throat. My vision blurred with tears as I focused on his faded orange jumpsuit.

"You know why." His eyes narrowed as he leaned closer, like he was going to whisper a secret to me, but I could only hear him through the receiver.

My chest tightened, and I forced back the tears that threatened to fall. "That's not fair, Brock. I'd do anything to take back what happened."

He shook his head, his eyebrows pulled together. "You're better off now." He smiled sadly. "No one can hurt my Bird."

"You killed them. You killed us."

"I think about you every second of every single day." His voice sounded wistful. We stared at each other for a long moment as a million things left unsaid passed between us. "That's my punishment. I get to spend eternity knowing I can't be with you."

"We could have had our forever, Brock."

His head dipped, and he ran his hand over the still-short buzz cut. "We never had forever, Lie."

"This wasn't supposed to happen." I shook my head as tears flowed over the apples of my cheeks.

"I'm sorry." He shook his head, his jaw clenched. "I'm so sorry, Bird."

My mind raced as I thought of all the kids in my school—of Shelly and Ms. Campbell.

"That day..." My words caught as I struggled to keep my composure.

His eyes glanced around and to the phone at my ear, like he was worried I'd say something that shouldn't be overheard. "That day is over now. You need to move on and try to..." He squeezed his eyes closed as he struggled to keep his composure. "Be happy, Bird."

I nodded, but the fear of that day was heavy in the air around me.

"It haunts me," I whispered.

"You have nothing to be scared of anymore. *You* are safe. They have their monster in a cage. No one can hurt you anymore.

You're free, Bird. I set you free." A tear ran down his face, and my hand twitched, wanting to wipe it away.

"Did you do it…on purpose? Did you mean to hurt me?" My voice was barely a whisper; I was terrified of his response.

Brock's face turned serious. "Never. I never would have hurt you, Bird."

"You did."

"Time's up," a guard yelled, startling me, and I jumped.

"I love you, Lie. I'm sorry." He stood, pushing back his chair.

"Brock, I forgive you."

He hung up the phone, his eyes lingering on me for an extra second before he was escorted away with the others.

I felt dazed as I stood from my chair and headed toward the exit. The door in front of me opened, and I smiled faintly to the guard as he nodded in return. I stepped through the last doorway and tilted my head up to the sky, my eyes closed, as I bathed in the fresh air and sunlight. I was free.

Strong arms wrapped around me from behind as I was lifted from the ground. I squealed, instantly feeling the tension ease from my shoulders in Abel's embrace. His lips came down to kiss me on the cheek before he lowered me to the ground.

"How do you feel?" he asked, as I spun around, looping my arms around his neck.

"Free."

His lips pressed against my forehead. "I love you so much, Kettle."

"Stop calling me that." His chest rumbled with laughter as I pulled back to admire his dimples. "I love you too, Abel."

"Forever?" His eyebrow cocked.

"Like I have a choice." I pulled his mouth to mine and kissed him.

"Cold-blooded, Kettle." He smacked me on the butt, which made me jump as I squealed. His hand grabbed mine, and he kissed the back of it as we made our way to his black Barracuda.

I slid into the passenger seat as I waited for him to join me. He got in, slamming the door and drumming his fingers on the steering wheel.

"What?" I asked him.

He smiled as he turned the key in the ignition, and the engine roared to life. He put the car in reverse, and dust swirled in a cloud around the car as we pulled out of the parking lot.

"I just wonder what things would have been like if we had met before." He let his thought hang in the air, and I imagined what life would have been like with Abel as I slung my arm out the window, letting my hand twist in the wind.

I took Abel's right hand in mine as I leaned back in my seat and propped my feet on the dashboard, my eyes scanning his perfect angelic face as my hair whipped around my face. "I think we were always meant to be, one way or another."

"Yeah?" He glanced at me with a crooked smile.

"Yeah." I pulled my bottom lip between my teeth. "You don't think so?"

He shrugged as he turned onto the highway, and we headed west. "I just don't know what I did to deserve you."

"I'm still trying to figure that out myself," I teased, as I leaned forward and turned up the radio.

He tugged on my hand, which made me fall on my side against him. "Come here, Kettle."

I wrapped my arms around his waist and closed my eyes as I squeezed him.

"So…what did you two talk about?" Abel cleared his throat, and I smiled against his side.

"You jealous?" I teased, as his arm tensed around me. "Don't be." I settled in tighter against him. "You're my forever. He was a lesson."

Abel's lips pressed against the top of my head as I felt the car turn a hard left.

"Whoa. Where are we going?"

"Hotel."

I sat up and pushed my hair from my face as I laughed at the sign. "Dead End Inn? Really?"

"You scared, Kettle?"

"Only of your sense of humor. Your jokes are going to bore me to death."

"Cute. You're real cute, Kettle. Now get out of the car."

"You're serious?"

His expression didn't change, and I groaned as I opened my door and stepped out of the car. He got out as well, and we both rounded the front.

"So you thought this would be…what? Romantic?" I asked him.

He chuckled as he draped his arm over my shoulders, and we headed toward the entrance. "There's someone here we're supposed to meet."

I looked at him confused, but I understood when he pulled open the door to the office. "Jesus," I mumbled, as I took in the scene. There was blood, black and dried, in splatters across the walls.

"No, not Jesus. This is Brandon. He was robbed a few hours ago." My body froze, and I pulled back against Abel's grip. "Be cool, Kettle. What am I saying? Be like me, Kettle."

"Oh…you got jokes?" I said. "You're seriously joking right now?"

"You're going to scare our new friend." He plastered a smile on his face, and his voice rose. "You all right, sir?"

"Help," a faint voice mumbled from behind the desk. I glanced at Abel before hurrying to the counter and bending over the edge to look down at a very badly injured Brandon.

"Is he...?" I asked, glancing back at Abel. He shook his head, and I let out a breath I didn't realize I'd been holding.

"He would be if we hadn't stopped here." Abel grabbed the phone on the counter and picked it up. "It's dead." He started to laugh but cleared his throat as I glared at him. "All right. That was lame." He pulled his cell from his pocket and dialed the police as I slipped around the counter and knelt next to the hotel owner.

"You're going to be OK." I tried to soothe him.

His bloodied hand wrapped around my arm. "Are you an angel?"

Abel snorted, and I glared up at him. "No. We're here to help you."

"Thank God," he murmured, and Abel rolled his eyes.

"Actually, my name is Abel, and this is Kettle," he began, but I interrupted.

"*Actually*, my name is Delilah. You're going to be just fine. You're real lucky we stopped in here." I brushed his graying hair from his forehead.

"It's a miracle. Bless you. Bless you."

Just when I thought Abel was going to die—a second time, for his not getting the credit for his miraculous save—we heard sirens in the distance, and I couldn't hold back the smile that spread over my face.

We waited for the paramedics to get closer before we slipped outside and into Abel's car. "Lesson of the day, dear Kettle, is that without whatever happened to us in the past, this guy wouldn't have been saved today."

"So…everything happens for a reason?" I asked, confused.

"No. Shit happens."

"Oh, that's poetic."

"But we saved his life, so it kind of makes it worth it, right?"

"I guess." I slid against his side as he pulled out of the parking lot and passed the ambulance and police cars that were on the side road.

"You guess?" He shook his head as he stepped on the gas, and we continued on our trip west, toward California. "Kettle, you're not embracing my awesome. Embrace the awesome."

"So are you going to tell me how you knew?" I pulled back to look at him, and his gaze flicked to mine.

"Well, I'd always had a feeling of awesome, even as a young boy."

"My God. You're infuriating."

"Kettle, I'm touched, but you don't need to call me 'God.'"

I shook my head. "You're so lucky I love you."

"I know. Trust me—I know." His tone was serious as he pressed a kiss into my hair. "I love you too, Delilah."

Happily ever afterlife.

CPSIA information can be obtained at www.ICGtesting.com
Printed in the USA
LVOW06s2031060514

384658LV00023B/398/P